Lesley is a retired head teacher and started writing for pleasure soon after retirement. She wrote most of the following stories during the lockdown, finding them very cathartic. Her interest in ghosts and the supernatural began when an aunt gave her a copy of Dickens' *A Christmas Carol* for her 12th birthday. She has read it every year since. Lesley has three daughters and lives in County Durham.

Table of Contents

A Christmas Gift	11
Matchmaker	21
Jojo	38
Brotherly Love	46
The Missing Patient	51
Retribution	62
At the Foot of the Stairs	71
The House at The Top Of the Cliff	83
The Rocking Chair	97
Good News	106
Premonition	113
Red Ribbons	124
Lily	140

I dedicate this book to my three lovely daughters, Louise, Kate and Rebekah, and to my dear friend, Anne, who inspired three of my ghosts.

Thank you for your love, support and encouragement.

Lesley Anne Wright

WINTER TALES

GHOST STORIES FOR THE WINTER FIRESIDE

AUSTIN MACAULEY PUBLISHERS™
LONDON * CAMBRIDGE * NEW YORK * SHARJAH

Copyright © Lesley Anne Wright 2023

The right of Lesley Anne Wright to be identified as author of this work has been asserted by the author in accordance with sections 77 and 78 of the Copyright, Designs and Patents Act 1988.

All rights reserved. No part of this publication may be reproduced, stored in a retrieval system, or transmitted in any form or by any means, electronic, mechanical, photocopying, recording, or otherwise, without the prior permission of the publishers.

Any person who commits any unauthorised act in relation to this publication may be liable to criminal prosecution and civil claims for damages.

This is a work of fiction. Names, characters, businesses, places, events, locales, and incidents are either the products of the author's imagination or used in a fictitious manner. Any resemblance to actual persons, living or dead, or actual events is purely coincidental.

A CIP catalogue record for this title is available from the British Library.

ISBN 9781398428362 (Paperback)
ISBN 9781398428379 (ePub e-book)

www.austinmacauley.com

First Published 2023
Austin Macauley Publishers Ltd®
1 Canada Square
Canary Wharf
London
E14 5AA

My thanks to all the team at Austin Macauley Publishers for their work in bringing this book to print.

A Christmas Gift

I was not looking forward to Christmas; on the contrary, I was very much dreading it. I feared that there would be too many ghosts of Christmases past and I had no hope of finding any cheer in a Christmas present. A lonely Christmas therefore, loomed before me, the rift with my one and only child a heavy burden. I do not wish to dwell on the causes of our separation; it was just one of those silly family squabbles that gets out of hand, until mountains have been made from molehills and angry, hurtful words that cannot be unsaid have been exchanged in heated arguments. We are too alike, my daughter and I, both stubborn, both refusing to admit fault, neither prepared to be the first to say, "I'm sorry."

In my melancholy mood, I had declined the kind invitations of friends and wider family; I was determined to wallow in my misery in a solitary fashion and so I had rented for myself a small cottage in a quiet village, several hours from home, where I would be in no danger of disturbance from well-meaning but unwelcome visitors. By Christmas Eve, I had been in the village for three days and that morning I'd awoken to see that a gentle snow had begun falling. The cottage was warm and welcoming enough and I had made some attempt at recognising the season; a small tree stood by the window, lights twinkling merrily, as if in an effort to dispel my gloom, in which endeavour it failed miserably. I had found fresh holly and ivy and these lay across the small mantel piece, where a fire blazed, the only other source of light in the room as the afternoon drew on towards dusk. I watched the snow gently falling for some time, lost in thoughts of other Christmas Eves, when I was a happy wife and mother. I recalled the faces of those whose absence I now so keenly felt; I closed my eyes and heard their laughter and my heart broke afresh. I had visited his grave before I left, laying fresh Christmas blooms; Tom had always loved Christmas, his inner child resurfacing each year at Christmastide. When our daughter was born, it only heightened for him the wonders and magic of it all. He revelled in it and happily, I caught his mood and joined in. They were happy times; we were content with each other and with the world.

The first Christmas without him was difficult; we two grieving souls did our best to console each other and to welcome the season as he would have wished us to, but in truth, neither of us had the heart for it. The year that followed mellowed our grief a little and as the second after we'd lost him year wore on, we began to look forward to the coming festivities. Yet, here I was, alone in a stranger's cottage, far from hearth and home. My daughter and I were estranged and my world had collapsed around me. I had no desire for Christmas and the memories it would bring.

The snow was falling more heavily now and the landscape began to take on the magical look of a Christmas card; even in my misery, I could acknowledge that much. I decided to go for a walk and finding boots, gloves and scarf, I put on my coat and ventured out into the village. In truth, I wished to escape the tree and the solitary gift beneath it, which bore the name of my beloved absent child. Locking the door, I turned left and walked away from the hub of the village and out towards the church, which I could see some distance off. I had made no conscious decision to walk to the church, rather my feet seemed to have a mind of their own. Upon reaching it, I stopped to admire the exquisitely carved woodwork of the lych-gate and I realised that there was a sizeable graveyard beyond too and I stood, silently for a few minutes, looking at the grave stones before me, thinking mournfully of the grave I'd visited only a few days earlier. I pushed open the gate and walked in to get a better look at the rather pretty church. It was not large, but was very pleasing to the eye. A sign told me it was the church of All Souls and that the vicar's name was The Reverend John Markham. There would be a carol evensong this evening at seven and then the traditional midnight service, neither of which I had any intention of attending.

I was not a church goer, as I was not a believer; that had been my husband's province and I had been happy enough for him to embrace his faith and all that it meant. I had looked on and smiled indulgently, gently fending off every attempt to convert me. I stood now, on the threshold of the little church of All Souls, undecided about going in. What would be my motive for doing so? To get out of the cold and warm through a little? I was no hypocrite, so it would not be to find solace or peace, no, not that. To admire the architecture and stained glass windows then, I told myself. I hesitated briefly and turned to look back at the graveyard. A shiver shook me violently and suddenly, I did indeed feel chilled through to the bone, recalling the old saying, 'Someone had walked over my grave.' Without further delay, I turned the heavy handle and pushed open the solid, wooden door, stepping into the tiny vestibule of the church, not at all surprised to find it unlocked and open to anyone wishing to enter. It was deadly quiet and though now out of the weather, it was also extremely cold. Gingerly, I opened the inner door and peered into the church. It was typical of small country churches everywhere. A central aisle split two rows of pews and I could see a baptismal font to one side of the altar ahead of me. Closing the door behind me, I walked down the aisle towards the font and altar, which was beautifully decorated with fresh, seasonal blooms. A Christmas tree stood at the other side, gaily decorated, although the lights were not switched on. A beautiful angel rested on top, wings outspread and hands folded as if in prayer.

I must have stood looking at the angel and the tree for several minutes, lost in thought for I was startled when a gentle voice said, "It's beautiful, isn't it?"

I had not realised I was no longer alone; I had not heard any approaching footsteps and I turned now to see a man, taller than me by several inches, standing beside me, also observing the angel.

"Yes, it is beautiful," I acknowledged.

"It's very old, well over a hundred years," my companion informed me, "it was a gift to the people of the parish."

"Oh, really?"

I could think of nothing more profound to say and truth to tell, I did not really wish to engage in small talk with this quiet stranger.

"Oh yes, a very special gift, given in thanks for help freely given during the season of peace and goodwill, on a night when the snow fell just as heavily as it does now and a stranger to our little village, found himself lost and in need, alone at Christmas."

He said no more, as if waiting for me to respond and after a few silent moments, I felt compelled to break the silence.

"How interesting," I remarked, "do you know the whole story?"

"I do indeed; everyone in Winterfield knows the legend of the angel. Shall we sit and I will tell you the whole of it?"

We sat on the pew directly in front of the tree and he continued the tale.

"The snow had been falling all that day and lay thickly along the lanes and hedgerows. It was a bad night for travellers to be out and about and one poor soul had lost his way in the whiteout. He related that he had been heading for a village which when he named it, he was told, was three miles further west but he had lost the road and he had felt very fortunate indeed to have stumbled upon the church in Winterfield. The evening service had just ended and it seemed the entire village spilled out from the church to wend their way home. The landlord of the Fox and Hounds offered to stable his horse and give him a room for the night, free of charge as it was Christmas, and in honour of that little family, who so long ago had sought shelter and found it in a stable. Gratefully, he warmed himself in front of the fire and over a few mugs of ale had joined in the locals' chatter. It transpired that they had been dismayed that evening to get to the service only to find that the tree was missing its little angel and that the top of the tree was bare. No one knew where it was to be found; the vicar had declared himself perplexed because, it had definitely been very carefully put away in its usual place on twelfth night, only twelve months previously."

"It was declared a mystery and the conversation then moved on to other, less perplexing topics. Unable to continue his journey for several more days, the traveller spent Christmas at Winterfield and although away from loved ones and worried that they must be in despair at his absence, he could only hope they would realise he had sought shelter from the weather and pray that they would soon be reunited and despite all this, his Christmas was a pleasant one, made so by the warm welcome he received from the villagers.

"This kindness was clearly not forgotten for several months later, when the snow was long thawed, the vicar received a parcel and inside was the very angel you see now, accompanied by a note which simply said, 'To the people of the Parish of Winterfield, in gratitude for your welcoming hospitality last Christmas to a stranger in need. May the spirit of Christmas always be present among you.' Legend now has it, that if a stranger comes amongst us and is in need, the angel will bestow on the stranger a Christmas gift."

My companion finished his tale and sat now, silently looking at the object of the story, as did I.

We sat there in companionable silence for a time until he turned to me once more and introduced himself as Michael Carter. I took his proffered hand, and told him my own name.

"Welcome to Winterfield, stranger," he replied, smiling at me warmly, "I must go now, my wife and son will be waiting for me. Matthew is almost three now and Joan finds him rather a handful at times. I promised I would not be out late tonight of all nights. Christmas is a time for family, don't you agree?

I'm sure you wish to be off home to your loved ones. Merry Christmas."

"Merry Christmas," I replied, turning again towards the angel, drawn by I knew not what, towards the angelic expression on the little face staring down at me from the top of the tree. When I turned back to watch my companion leave, he had already disappeared from sight, as silently as he had come. *Strange,* I thought, *that his shoes made no noise on the tiled floor, as mine had done.* I remained only a few moments more thinking, somewhat sceptically, about the tale I had just heard and what kind of gifts the angel was said to bestow, as this particular had not been mentioned and then I too, left the church and made my way out into the graveyard.

It was snowing less heavily now but it was growing quite dark and before the light disappeared completely, as I made my way down the path to the gate, I stopped to read the inscriptions on several headstones, still just visible in the darkening gloom. I was struck by a particular monument, possibly because of the subject of my conversation in the church. It was a beautiful angel, carved it seemed to me, from the purest white marble, which had stood the test of time and all manner of weather; its head was bowed and inclined slightly to one side and it appeared to be looking down at the grave, as if in silent watch over the dead below. It's cold, marble hands were joined as in prayer and its wings were outspread, like those of the angel on the tree. It was ethereally beautiful and I studied it wistfully for several moments before I turned my attention to the inscription below. I cannot now describe to you, the sensation I felt when I read the words engraved on that headstone.

Carter

Here lies Joan, beloved wife of Michael

Born 28 June 1900, died 24 December 1923

And their much-loved son, Matthew

Born 31 December 1920, died 24 December 1923

Michael

Born 14 August 1898, died 17 May 1979

Rooted to the spot and oblivious to the cold, overtaken by an overwhelming sadness, I stared at the words, reading them over and over, until, for the second time that day, I was startled by a voice at my side.

"Good evening."

I turned to see a man, who judging by the collar he was wearing, was clearly the vicar.

"Have you come for the evening service?"

I could not immediately speak and I could hear the concern in his voice as he asked me if I was feeling unwell. I managed to shake my head and he took me gently by the arm and bade me back inside the church, where he urged me to sit down while he fetched me a glass of water. Quietly, he took his place beside me and soon enough, I was more settled and able to relate to him the meeting I'd had in the very spot in which we two now sat. He listened without comment until I had related the entire encounter and then, gently he took my hand.

"Ah," he murmured, "you are a stranger come to Winterfield and you are in need in some way."

I stared at him, stupefied but before I could say anything, he began to tell me Michael's own sad story. On Christmas

Eve in 1923, Michael Carter had been to the evening service, his wife and young son remaining at home as the little one had a cold. During the service, while most of the village was in the little church, the Carter's cottage had burned to the ground and both his wife and child had died, overcome by smoke. For several years after, Michael had refused to celebrate Christmas, until the night before Christmas Eve about four years after the tragedy, a young woman arrived in the village, having taken a wrong turning. It was growing late and she had stopped to ask Michael if she would find a room anywhere, not wishing to continue her journey alone and in worsening weather.

"The rest, as they say, is history," he concluded, "they were married the following year. Her gravestone lies beside the one you were looking at just now. Michael had requested he be buried with his first wife and son and she ensured his final wish was carried out. They never had children of their own but Ellen saved Michael; she gave him a reason to live again. Another Christmas gift bestowed by our angel. Ellen had the monument erected after his burial."

I could not speak for several moments until, finally I managed to utter, "You mean, I was speaking with a ghost? With Michael Carter's ghost?"

He did not immediately reply, merely shrugging his shoulders but his smile led me to believe that he clearly believed it and then he said, "The angel has bestowed many gifts, all different in nature."

I looked at him and smiled back; now I understood why I had heard neither his approach nor his leaving and only now did I recall the rather old fashioned attire, the strange manner of speech. Now I understood the purpose of his coming and of our conversation, here before the Christmas angel in the little church of All Souls.

"Thank you," I told the Reverend Markham, shaking his hand, "I think I understand it all and what I must do. I cannot stay for the evensong but I will return later for the midnight service."

My earlier resolve not to acknowledge Christmas, completely forgotten. Once more, I left the church and as I walked past the angel, eternally watching over Michael and his family, I murmured a silent 'thank you'.

Taking my phone from my pocket, I selected the required number and when I heard her beloved voice, I smiled as I said, "Merry Christmas, darling, it's Mum."

Matchmaker

Harvey sat in bemused silence, or possibly shock, depending on your knowledge or otherwise of doggy psychology, his head cocked to one side, his liquid brown eyes following every move Martha made. The bedroom was a mess, as was the living room and indeed the kitchen. The remnants of a relationship lay strewn about in the various rooms, CDs shattered, their cases no longer required, were piled in every available waste bin, although naturally, Martha had taken great care to save her own personal favourites. Photos of a once happy couple, were ripped to shreds and likewise had been consigned to the bins. The few clothes he had not already removed were in a bin bag, either to be taken to a charity shop or else to join the other rubbish.

Her rampage, having already lasted almost twenty minutes, was now burning itself out, and exhausted Martha sat down on the bed next to her half packed suitcase. Sadly, she surveyed the carnage she had created and a silent tear first welled and then, slowly made its way down her cheek. Harvey, who had until now, sat as still as a statue, quietly stood and went to his mistress, gently laying his head on her lap, before licking up the tears that had found their way to her hand.

"I hate him, Harvey, and I hate her more," Martha told him, "how could they do this to me? I've given him two years of my life and she's supposed to be my best friend and they do this to me three weeks before Christmas. He's a bastard and she's a bitch and I'll never forgive either of them."

Of course Harvey had absolutely no idea what his mistress was saying – well, why would he, being a one year old Wirehaired Fox Terrier? He understood commands such as sit, come, fetch but he was not able to piece together full sentences, as intelligent as he was. However, he was keenly aware that this was not the mistress he knew and loved. Something was wrong and his little face, with the rather fetching eye patch, would have shown his bewilderment and concern if he'd been at all capable. Instead, he remained by her side, patiently waiting for her next move.

"Well, boy, I'm almost finished packing and then we'll be off."

Martha stood and looked down at the suitcase. She had thrown things in rather absentmindedly and now stopped to give it some thought. She hadn't really decided on how long she'd be away, all she knew was that she could not face Christmas here, with reminders of Jonathan and the life together he'd so carelessly cast aside for her so called friend, Gemma. She couldn't face the commiserations of other friends and going to parties and socialising over the festive period as a recently dumped singleton, was simply out of the question. She folded several more jumpers and two more pairs of jeans into the case and slammed it shut. She'd decide on timescales later, if and when she was feeling a little better. That was the beauty of being a freelance writer; as long as she had her laptop with her, she could work just as well away from home, as in it.

"Come on, boy, time to go," she informed Harvey, who obediently followed her from the room.

Setting the case down in the hallway, she put on Harvey's harness and carried him to the car. Once he was safely fastened into the back seat, she fetched the case and her handbag and closing the door on the mess, she got into the car without looking back.

It was growing dark and everywhere she looked, windows were lit up with twinkling Christmas lights. Tears threatened again, but angrily, she fought them back and concentrated on the road ahead. Willow Cottage was two hours' drive away and she needed to keep her mind on the road. Even so, she couldn't stop herself from going over the day's events. Was it really only this morning that Jonathan had dropped his bombshell? A few, short hours ago she had been happy, one half of a couple who had talked of plans to marry, have children, move from her little flat to a house with a garden and now, here she was, driving to Cumbria, to the little cottage her parents had bought years ago as a holiday let. Her mum and dad had been so concerned, telling her that she should come home to Kent, but she had told them that she needed time to be alone and that she simply couldn't face Christmas right now; she'd reassured them that Willow Cottage was just what she needed for the time being. Maybe, if she felt up to it, she'd be home on Christmas Eve. Her parents hadn't pushed it; they knew their daughter well enough to know when she'd made up her mind and so, her dad had simply told her he'd ring Mrs Jenkins at the Post Office, asking her to leave some provisions in the fridge and to turn on the heating. Martha had thanked him quietly and telling them she loved them, rang off.

Determined to concentrate on the journey ahead and to put all thoughts of Jonathan out of her mind, she drove out of Durham and turned onto the A1 South. The motorway was reasonably quiet and thirty-five minutes later she was on the A66 heading towards Cumbria.

"Fingers crossed, we'll be in Hoxton by about nine, Harvey," she told her silent companion, who in fact was fast asleep.

Martha turned on the radio and as Classic FM broke the silence, she pushed down on the accelerator and listened as the strains of The Coventry Carol filled the car. An hour and forty-five minutes later, she was turning towards Hoxton which was now only ten minutes away.

The village was quiet and Martha saw no one out and about as she drove past the village green towards Willow Cottage, which lay at the far end of the village, beyond the The King's Head pub, all lit up and cheerily festive, and then was soon turning onto the driveway of a pretty little cottage with a small front garden, visible thanks to someone having switched on the porch light; *Mrs Jenkins, bless her,* Martha assumed. She decided to take Harvey for a walk before unpacking the car.

He'd probably be in need of one by now, and she reached for his lead on the seat beside her before announcing, "We're here, boy; let's go for a walk and stretch ourselves."

As she fastened his lead, Harvey did indeed stretch and yawn and then was suddenly wide awake and eager to be out of the car.

"Hey, slow down, boy, there's no hurry!"

Harvey begged to disagree and pulled Martha towards the village green, in the middle of which was a single, large oak tree, just waiting for Harvey to water it, which he duly did and then, business done he seemed content to allow Martha to decide where they would go next.

Martha, decided to walk back towards the pub, mainly because the road out past Willow Cottage would be dark, leading as it did, down away from the village, to the river and into open countryside. *The pub would have its usual customers, although being a Wednesday, it would probably be rather quiet,* she thought. The few, small properties that lay between Willow Cottage and the pub, were displaying their Christmas lights and several had not drawn curtains, so that their Christmas trees were visible to anyone passing by. Wistfully, Martha stopped and gazed at the last one before The King's Head. Like Willow Cottage, it was detached, traditional but in stark contrast to Willow Cottage, it was gaily lit up, a big wreath on the front door and the window almost entirely filled with a large tree, beautifully decorated, it's lights blinking on and off in a steady rhythm. *Perfect for a Christmas card, if only there was some snow,* Martha mused as her eyes filled yet again. Angrily, she brushed the tears away, turning away from the festive spectacle, back towards the pub.

Harvey obediently trotted on beside her, until just as they reached the pub, a noisy group came towards them, clearly heading for the warmth and cheer of the interior. Harvey immediately sat down and barked loudly at the on-comers.

"Harvey, no!"

Martha shushed him.

Most of the group barely glanced at them but one tall straggler stopped, bent down, tickled Harvey behind his ear and said, "Hey, boy, are we making too much noise?"

"I'm sorry," Martha apologised, "he's not usually so averse to a bit of chatter. Maybe it's because we're in a strange place. He at least hasn't been here before."

"Just visiting, are you?" the tall, decidedly handsome stranger asked.

"At Willow Cottage; we've just arrived," Martha explained.

"Well, it's nice to meet you…"

"Martha, and this is Harvey."

Martha filled in the blanks for him.

"I'm Jack; welcome to Hoxton. Hope we bump into each other again," he said reaching out to shake Martha's hand.

How very quaint, Martha mused as they shook hands and said their goodbyes, *he's very polite and formal and rather good looking, although of course,* she chided herself, *I'm not the least bit interested in that!*

Tired now, Martha led Harvey in a quick circuit of the village green and back towards Willow Cottage. Fifteen minutes later, her bags had been deposited at the foot of the stairs and she was in the kitchen spooning dog food into a bowl. While Harvey demolished his meal, she checked the fridge and found eggs, bacon, cheese, butter and milk.

"Thank you, Mrs Jenkins." Martha offered silent thanks to her benefactor, as she set about making herself an omelette.

The white wine she'd also found in the fridge, was deliciously chilled and she enjoyed the familiar taste of a good Chablis as it slid down her throat. Several glasses of wine and a cheese omelette later, Martha took her bags upstairs to the larger of the two bedrooms and began to unpack the few belongings she'd brought with her. She was really tired now, the shock of this morning's events, the drive and the wine were all taking effect. She decided on a quick bath and then bed.

With Harvey settled in his own cosy, little bed beside hers, she climbed beneath the duvet and tried to read, something she always did before sleep but she simply couldn't concentrate and having read the same line more than once, she gave up, switched off the lamp on the bedside table and lay down. It was now that she recalled how, as a child when here in the cottage, she had been convinced it was haunted. Back then, she had been in the smaller back bedroom and she was utterly convinced that there was someone else in the room with her. Her father had to check under the bed, in the wardrobe and behind the drawn curtains in order to convince her she was quite alone. Of course, she hadn't been convinced. It was just that Dad couldn't see what or who was there because, well, you can't always see ghosts, now can you? She recalled that it was always just as she was dozing off, that she would feel the slightest touch of her hair and smell the faintest whiff of perfume. It was oddly comforting. She lay quietly in the dark, listening for the slightest sound, waiting for that familiar feeling of another presence but there was nothing to concern her and Harvey was quietly snoring already. Surely he would sense if something was amiss? Reassured, she was soon asleep and despite the trauma of being dumped by the man she had thought loved her and betrayed by her so called best friend, she slept peacefully, awaking the next morning refreshed and alert.

"Morning, boy," she said, stretching and expecting Harvey to jump on the bed and lick her in his usual excited manner but when she looked down at his bed, it was empty. "Harvey, here, boy. Where are you? You'd better not be up to mischief," she called aloud and putting on her dressing gown, she went to look for him.

She found him in the kitchen, sitting in front of the Aga, his little head moving from side to side, the way it did when something interesting had grabbed his attention or when he was listening to something. She stood in the doorway for several seconds and then he let out a single bark and turned to greet her, his tail wagging, obviously at ease and pleased to see her.

How did you get out, boy? She pondered, *I could swear the door was shut.*

Shrugging it off, she fed him, made herself poached eggs on toast and a cup of coffee and sat down to plan her day. *Shopping first,* she thought, needing to add to the meagre contents of the fridge-freezer and cupboards. After that, she'd need to do some work. She had a magazine article to complete and the deadline was now less than a week away. She anticipated she would be finished well before but she wanted to leave nothing to chance and besides, it would keep her mind off them.

Several hours later, she climbed out of the car and began to unload her shopping. The weather was good, cold but fine and once she had put the shopping away, she would take Harvey for a walk and then spend the afternoon at her laptop. She unloaded the last bag and kicking the front door shut behind her, she began to stash her groceries away. It was several minutes later that she heard a loud yelp, accompanied by a crash and an expletive from a clearly shocked man. She raced to the front door, which was now standing wide open and saw to her horror that Jack, that nice chap from the night before, had fallen from his bike and Harvey was sitting in the road too, clearly hurt and distressed.

"Oh, God, I'm so sorry," she said, "I could have sworn I shut the front door behind me. Are you hurt?"

"Only my male pride," Jack said ruefully, as he dusted himself down, "I think Harvey got the worst of it."

Jack quickly examined Harvey and then gently picking him up, he walked purposefully up the garden path.

"Bring my bike into the garden, please," he called over his shoulder.

Gently placing Harvey on the table, he set about examining him more closely.

"Broken leg, I suspect. It'll need an X-ray to confirm but I'm afraid there'll be no walks for a while, poor lad. Come to think of it, I might give my lunch-time ride a miss for a while and stick to the gym. It might be safer," he said, smiling at her.

Martha returned his smile, which left her feeling rather weak at the knees.

He's incredibly good looking, she thought before managing to stutter, "You seem very sure about his leg, but I'll take him to a vet and have him checked thoroughly."

Jack laughed and smiled at her again, his eyes twinkling, clearly amused.

"I am the vet," he said, "but no offence taken!"

Martha blushed to her roots and sputtered her apologies, stating once more that she could have sworn the front door was firmly closed.

"No harm done, except maybe to my bike but nothing that can't be fixed," Jack said, smiling that disarming smile at her.

"That's the second time today he's managed to escape," she said, explaining about the bedroom door as she made coffee and produced a plate of ginger biscuits and shortbread.

"Clever boy."

Jack laughed.

"But I can't imagine why he'd want to escape from you," he said and tickled Harvey's ear.

Martha blushed again. *I think he's flirting with me,* she thought to herself and found the idea rather pleasing. Jack had managed to fashion a splint and after they'd finished their coffee, Jack carried Harvey to Martha's car for the drive to his surgery.

"You know, if you wanted to see me again, you didn't have to attempt to kill me," he said, laughing.

Martha laughed at his teasing but repeated her apologies.

"I don't know how he's doing it," she said, "he's never managed to open closed doors before and now he's done it twice in one morning!"

An X-ray confirmed Jack's diagnosis and Harvey was duly sedated while a cast was put on and they then made the return journey to Martha's, Jack having cleared his absence for a while with his partner. Over yet another coffee, Jack asked why she was in the village so close to Christmas. Not feeling ready to tell anyone she had been so humiliated by recent events, she told him she had a deadline to meet and needed peace and quiet to get finished on time. Well, this wasn't exactly a lie now, was it? She did have a deadline; it just wasn't the primary cause of her arrival at the cottage. If he realised this, he didn't let it show. He was too busy admiring the silky, blonde curls falling loosely around her shoulders, the violet eyes, long lashed and large, the pretty, full rosebud lips. For her part, she was trying hard not to notice his strong, handsome face, those velvety brown eyes, and oh so kissable mouth. Each had noticed the absence of a ring on that finger. Harvey, for his part, lay quietly on his bed by the Aga, watching as things unfolded and heaved a huge sigh of satisfaction. He had played his part rather well.

"Do you like a quiz?" Jack was asking now. "It's quiz night tonight. An extra brain is always welcome in Team Brainbox. The more, the merrier."

"OK."

She found herself agreeing, although truth to tell, she hadn't really ever taken to pub quizzes.

"Sounds like fun. What time should I be there?"

"Quiz starts at eight but come for seven-thirtyish. See you then. I'd better get back to surgery. I'm neutering a beagle at three."

"Shhh!"

She admonished him.

"Do you want Harvey to hate you for ever more?"

"Heaven forfend!" he said, hands up in mock horror, "I need to keep in his mistress's good books."

He winked at her, tickled Harvey under his chin and left, in a draft of rather pleasant aftershave. It was as she was washing up that she caught the faintest smell of yet another scent, a flowery one, one she was sure she recognised but couldn't quite pin down.

"Odd," she said aloud and then thought no more about it.

The quiz turned out to be fun. Martha liked the company she found herself in. Besides Jack, the 'team' consisted of his mates, Sam and Luke and Luke's girlfriend, Jen. They didn't win but came a worthy second and she was pleased that she had contributed several very good answers. Jack walked her home afterwards and when she invited him in for a drink, he readily accepted. Harvey seemed pleased enough to see him, despite their earlier unfortunate encounter. Martha poured Jack a whisky and herself a white wine and Jack carried Harvey into the cosy living room. He kept Harvey on his knee, stroking and tickling him which he clearly enjoyed but as Martha informed him, he lapped up any attention no matter who from.

"Still," she said, "you must love animals to have devoted all those years of study to become a vet."

"I grew up on a farm," he told her, "my brother runs it, now that Dad's retired, but yes, I grew up surrounded by animals. Funnily enough though, I never wanted to be a farmer like Dad or Tom. I love being a vet, it's what I always wanted to do. Richard, my partner and I set up our practice three years ago. It's doing really well. What about you?" he asked, "I know you said you're a freelance writer but – and I hope you don't mind me saying this – but I get the feeling you're not just here to get your work finished."

Martha hesitated briefly but then looked at the earnest concern on Jack's face and told him the whole story.

"God, that's shitty," he said, "he doesn't deserve you and she was clearly no friend. It may not seem like it just now, but you're better off without both of them."

Martha nodded. After all, this was exactly what she'd told herself and despite the pain and humiliation of the betrayal, she knew that Jack was right. She would get over it and sooner than she might have hoped, she thought now, smiling at Jack and Harvey, who were clearly quite enamoured of one another. Jack had left after he'd asked her if she'd like to go out to dinner on Saturday evening. She'd readily agreed and as she was getting ready for bed, she felt happier than she had since the bombshell had dropped only the day before. It was just as she was nodding off that she imagined she felt the slightest brush of something against her brow and caught the faint smell of that perfume.

Her mood lifted in the coming days. She and Jack enjoyed each other's company and were spending more and more time together, although she had made it clear she wanted to take things slowly. She wasn't ready to rush things given the last disastrous romance, although her instincts told her Jack would never behave in such an appalling manner. At the end of her second week in the cottage, her mood so much lighter, she decided to put up the Christmas decorations. Harvey had lain on the sofa, watching as she decorated the tree, the mantelpiece and put up little statues of deer, snow topped houses and other little bits and pieces around the cottage. She crossed her fingers as she switched on the lights but to her delight, they sprang into life, twinkling merrily. She stood back to admire her efforts, feeling distinctly festive.

"I can't believe it's only two weeks since I was dumped!" she said to Harvey, watching the familiar tilt of his head as he listened.

She smiled at him.

"Who'd have thought it? I'm glad to be rid of them and I'm not going to waste any more of my precious time thinking about them. I won't let those two liars spoil Christmas for me."

Her dad had rung her several times begging her to come home for Christmas but she'd gently refused, reassuring him that she was fine, had made new friends and that she'd like to stay in the cottage until the new year. Reluctantly he had stopped pressing her and said she could have the cottage as long as she liked. He and her mum would hope to see her very soon. She'd met her deadline with a few days to spare and she'd decided to give herself a little holiday until after Christmas. Harvey was still unable to walk so she spent her days listening to her favourite music, reading and cleaning while her evenings were either spent with Jack and the others in the pub or else they'd eat supper and watch TV together as often as Jack's schedule allowed. As time passed, just as she promised herself, she found herself thinking less and less of the trauma that had brought her here in the first place and thanked her lucky stars that fate – and Harvey – had introduced her to Jack. Every now and then, she would smell that sweet scent and before sleep feel the gentle brush of something on her brow. It didn't worry her as it might once have done and in fact, she began to find it rather comforting, just as she used to as a child. From time to time, she would catch Harvey cocking his little head from side to side as if listening to something she couldn't hear. More than once it crossed her mind that she had been right as a child and that the cottage did indeed have a ghost. If there was a ghost here, she decided, it was definitely a friendly one.

Jack had invited her and Harvey to the farm for Christmas lunch. She was grateful for the friendly welcome of Tom, his wife Sally, their raucous, overly excited children, Nathan and Dominic and his parents, elderly but very much ready to join in the festivities and indulge their grandchildren. The day was perfect and it was as Jack drove them home that she made the decision that would change her life for ever. She could hardly believe that in the space of three weeks she had decided on such a momentous change.

"But nothing ventured, nothing gained," she told herself.

"Hi, Dad," she said, without preamble, "what would you say if I asked to rent the cottage on a more permanent basis? I know it would mean you losing the holiday let but I would pay the going rate."

"It was always going to be yours in any case," he told her, "this just brings things forward a touch. Of course you can, love. It's yours."

Martha smiled as she imagined her dad's loving face as he'd readily agreed to her request and made him promise they'd come and visit in the new year. She wanted her parents to meet Jack, although she kept this to herself for the time being. As she rang off and filled the kettle to make herself a cup of coffee, she caught the faintest whiff of perfume and she could have sworn she heard just the briefest of sighs.

She smiled, switched on the kettle and said to Harvey, "I think our ghost approves, boy. I can't wait to tell Jack that we're staying. I hope he approves too."

If Harvey had been able to speak, which would have been remarkable indeed, he would have told her that everything she said was true.

Rosie had listened to the phone call with approval. She smiled, unseen as Martha rang off and filled the kettle to make coffee. She winked at Harvey conspiratorially. They'd done it. It had all been rather easy in the end. Rosie remembered Martha as a child. She had frightened the child at first, although she'd only ever meant to take care of her, watch over her as she had done her own brood, here in this very cottage. She remembered clearly, as if it were yesterday, the day Bill had carried her, a twenty-year-old bride over the threshold and here they'd made a life together, raised three children, been happy. She had absolutely loved this cottage because she had raised her children here, Bill had been here, they had lived their whole married life here and when her time had come she had promised Bill that she would never leave him. She kept her promise. He would often smell her perfume, that floral one she always wore and be comforted. When his time came, two short years after he lost her, she knew he didn't want to stay, that he could let go and embrace his eternal rest but not her. She liked the coming and goings of the people who came after them and she'd stayed, not minding sharing the cottage with various holiday visitors but she especially liked it when Martha and her mum and dad were there. She'd been sad and concerned for Martha when she'd arrived at the beginning of December and she'd been determined to help her move on from her pain as quickly as possible. Over the years she'd grown adept at opening doors, moving things about, all unseen. She'd never once manifested herself as a visible being. She remained invisible, always. She moved about the cottage silently, the only mark of her presence her unmistakable scent, the slightest touch which felt almost like a gentle breeze. It was Rosie that had let Harvey out of the bedroom and Rosie that had opened the front door too, just as Jack had ridden by on his bike. She had first seen Jack when he'd visited a convalescing Labrador the previous spring. She'd liked him immediately. Here was a good, decent man, just the kind to help Martha forget her heartache. Yes, it had all been rather easy in the end. A helpful Fox Terrier and an open door at just the right moment. Rosie smiled, winked at her co-conspirator, funnily enough, the only one who could see her and ever so gently kissed the top of Martha's head as she sat, drinking her coffee and dreaming of a future in Hoxton, in her cottage, with Jack.

Jojo

I must have been eight or nine when I first learned about our family's dark past. Like any other curious child, fascinated and horrified in equal measure, I had read the details over and over, until the facts of the story were memorised but it was not long before I lost interest and it became a forgotten tale, stored away and never revisited.

I hadn't thought of the story for many years but now, I was twenty and in my second year at university, far away from home and having the time of my life. I'd made new friends and although studying hard for my degree in history, I was also playing hard and my social life was full and exciting, nights spent in the uni bar, talking, laughing, drinking until we had finally had enough and would stumble home, drunk but happy.

It was after one such night, tipsy and relaxed that my three housemates and I were chatting noisily about the usual girly stuff, boys, clothes, music and makeup. The house was large and old, Victorian I think and we each had a room of our own but we were good mates and we'd spend a lot of time in the large, communal kitchen. Now, as usual, we were sitting around the kitchen table, drinking cheap lager when Jenna asked if any of us had heard any strange noises or felt anything unusual.

"I'm telling you," she said seriously, "this house has more occupants than just us four!"

We laughed but I was curious and wanted to hear more and asked her to describe exactly what she meant. After all, we'd been here for three months and this was the first time she'd mentioned it. I consider myself a pretty down to earth character. I'm not given to flights of fancy. I like dealing with the facts. I like certainty, what can be proven, so I'm afraid I was highly sceptical of Jenna's noises but she was clearly rattled so I encouraged her to explain what it was that was bothering her.

"I keep feeling as if I'm being watched and I've heard footsteps on the stairs when I know for a fact I'm the only one home," she explained. "I thought at first I was imagining things but it's happened on a few occasions now. Haven't any of you heard anything?"

The three of us shook our heads and I watched as Jenna's face fell.

"I'm not making this up, guys," she said now, "really, this is real."

"Hey," I responded, "we're not saying it's not real, just that none of us has heard or felt anything. Why haven't you told us sooner?" I asked.

"Because I know how crazy it sounds and I didn't want you all to think I'm nuts!"

"Well, I think it's cool that we live in a haunted house."
Cathy laughed.

"I'd love to have a ghostly experience! Proof that life goes on, that's there more than just this life once we're six feet under."

"I'm not sure I would," Diane said, as she shivered violently, "and I'm not sure I like the idea of this house having its very own ghost either. How about you, Mel?"

"I think it depends on the ghost."

I laughed.

"If it's a mean dude, no but not all ghosts are supposed to be scary, are they? To be honest, I don't believe in ghosts. There'll be a perfectly rational explanation. This is an old house. Old houses make noises. There are bound to be creaks and groans."

"Well, I want to find out for sure," Jenna said, "why's it only me that can hear and feel stuff? This is more than the noises an old house makes. I know what that is and this is not it. What can we do? Call in a priest or something?"

"We could use a Ouija board," I suggested.

The others looked at me, shocked but I pressed on.

"Oh, come on, girls, it's only a bit of fun. You don't really think we're going to conjure up our ghost, do you? I'm sure there's a perfectly logical explanation for the noises you're hearing, Jenna. Come on, it'll be good for a laugh."

They looked at each other and then back at me and before I knew it, we were planning a seance for the next night, a Saturday. It was just going to be us four and we'd hold it right here in our kitchen at midnight. It absolutely had to be midnight, I insisted, the witching hour! We were all agreed on that. I promised I'd cut out the letters, words and numbers we'd need and the only other things required were a glass and some candles.

I woke up the following morning with a banging headache but several large glasses of water and a couple of painkillers later, I sat down at the table and began writing out, in dark black felt tip pen, the letters, numbers and words we'd need that night. This was not something I'd ever done before but I'd read about it, seen films and TV programmes. I didn't give any credence to the dire warnings I'd also heard about Ouija boards being dangerous, inviting in unwanted spirits, opening portals that can't then be closed. As far as I was concerned, this was all just a bit of fun and I was sure it would prove to Jenna that our house was not haunted. The others were still sleeping and I left them to it as I gathered a few candles, made sure we had some booze and nibbles and then went back to my room to lie down as my head was still aching. I fell asleep and didn't wake again until well into the afternoon, a calm, dreamless sleep, just as always. I didn't see the others until early evening as they too had been sleeping off the night before. Everyone was still agreed that we would hold our seance and we decided that just for once we'd stay sober long enough to carry through our plans. We talked about ghosts and whether or not we each believed in them. I repeated that I definitely didn't. Jenna said she was inclined to think she did; how else could she explain what she was experiencing? She refused to believe it was just the house making noises. The others weren't sure but we all agreed that we enjoyed a good, scary story, even me. There's nothing quite like being scared out of your wits by a really good ghost, we decided.

Just before midnight, we all gathered around the table. It was completely dark outside and with only a few candles flickering, it was suitably atmospheric, creepy almost. I had arranged the letters, numbers and the YES and NO in a circle and placed a small glass upside down in the centre.

We each placed a forefinger on top of the glass and I said, "Is anybody there? Do you have a message for anyone here?"

Nothing happened and Cathy giggled.

"Shush, Cathy," Jenna said crossly, "nothing will happen if we don't take it seriously. Go on, Mel, try again."

"Hello, is there anybody there? Please speak to us. Do you have a message for anyone here?" I repeated.

Suddenly, the candles flickered wildly, in spite of there being no breath of air in the room and then the glass moved slowly, ever so slowly across the table towards the YES.

"Who did that?" Diane, clearly shaken, demanded, "who pushed the glass?"

We all looked at each other, our faces eerily illuminated by the candlelight. I shook my head and both Jenna and Cathy did the same.

"Hello, welcome," I said, "do you have a message for one of us?" The glass moved backwards ever so slightly and then shot sharply to the YES again.

"Who is the message for?" I asked, and the glass moved again, gathering pace but none of it made sense.

It shot from letter to letter but spelled nothing out. If there was a spirit in the glass, which I seriously doubted, convinced it was one of the others moving it, it clearly understood yes and no but perhaps that was the limit of its ability to communicate.

"Let's try just asking it yes or no questions," I suggested. "Are you able to read and write?" I asked, watching carefully to see if I could make out whose hand was pushing the glass across the table.

The glass moved rapidly back to the YES.

"Can you spell your name?" I asked.

The glass moved again and I watched, as it spelled out a name; JOJO. JOJO. JOJO. Three times in rapid succession it spelled out its name. Only now, did I begin to feel a sense of unease and a shiver crept up my spine. I tried to recall where I had heard that name before.

"Are you here for, Jenna?" Jenna asked the glass, getting a negative response.

The others asked the same question with the same reply until finally it was my turn but of course we all knew by then that it was me who the spirit had come for. And then, from the back of my memory I remembered the name Jojo and where I had first come across it.

"Are you from Jamaica?" I asked.

YES.

"Were you a slave?"

YES.

"Why are you here?" I said now.

"That's not a yes or no question," Cathy whispered.

"Can you tell us why you're here?" I repeated, ignoring Cathy.

Slowly, the glass began moving from letter to letter and Diane spoke the words the glass spelled out.

"I did it. Sorry."

The glass stopped and there was no further movement. We sat in silence for several long seconds and the glass moved again.

"Forgive me."

I gasped now and stood up abruptly, knocking the glass flying and swiping my hand across the table, scattering the letters. The others looked at me, clearly shocked.

"What the fuck?" Cathy said.

I was shivering now, I felt cold from head to foot, despite the heating.

Shaking my head, I managed to blurt out, "We can't do this. It's over, we have to stop."

And turning, I fled from the kitchen.

The others followed me into my bedroom and as I sat, still shaking from head to toe, Diane came and sat down on the bed, beside me. She put her arms around me, saying nothing while the others looked at me, clearly concerned. No one spoke for several minutes, until finally I began to calm down and felt more like my normal self.

"What happened back there?" Diane said, "Can you tell us? Do you want to talk about it?"

I paused for a few seconds.

"I think I know who your ghost is, Jenna and if I say he's forgiven, he'll go away and we'll be left alone," I said.

They all looked at me as if it was me who'd gone mad now.

"You don't believe in ghosts," Cathy reminded me.

"I didn't but then I'd never experienced one, never had proof before," I said and then I told them the story I had read all those years ago in my grandmother's attic.

I had found a newspaper article, very old and faded. It was about the sudden death of Charles Osbourne, a distant relative. He had owned a sugar plantation in Jamaica, along with almost two hundred slaves who worked on it. Apparently, he was a violent, cruel man. His slaves were regularly beaten, humiliated and over worked. I remember feeling angry and ashamed that we were related, even though I was very young at the time. The report told how on one night during a storm, his horse had come home alone. A search was immediately conducted but it wasn't until the following morning that his body was found. His injuries were extensive and he had sustained a deep head wound. It was, the coroner stated, impossible that a fall from his horse would have been the cause of such wounds. It finished by stating that the slave who had accompanied him had also not returned home that night and had clearly absconded. A huge search party was arranged and it was several days before he had been recaptured. He was subsequently charged with the wilful murder of his master and duly hanged. The slave's name was JOJO.

Brotherly Love

Matthew peered out of the curtain less window at the stars, clearly visible in the cloudless night sky and let the tears slide unchecked, down his cheeks and onto his pillow. He lay quite still, not wanting to disturb his sleeping brother whose slow, rhythmic breathing he could hear next to him in the small bed they shared. He replayed the evening's conversation over and over in his mind and his stomach lurched each time he thought of the coming horror. He couldn't do it, he simply couldn't. The terror of it gripped him and the nausea swept over him afresh. No matter what his friends would think of him, no matter that they would laugh and taunt him, calling him sissy and a coward. No matter that his father would be ashamed of him, possibly disown him, while his mother would be disappointed and afraid for him; he simply couldn't do it. Only Eddie, his elder by three minutes knew his terrible, shameful secret. Only Eddie had understood his horrified silence and had extended his comforting hand under the table as their father had made his pronouncement. The day had been like many other days before it; there had been nothing that would have set it apart from any other, until his father had delivered his shocking news over their evening meal of broth and bread.

I'll run away, he thought now, *I'll run away and never come back. Anything, anything would be better than the darkness and claustrophobia of the mine that lurked menacingly at the edge of their village and where his grandfather, father, uncles and cousins all toiled beneath the earth and where their father had announced they too, must now do their bit.*

"Well, lads," he'd proclaimed matter of factly, "you're twelve at the end of this week and old enough now to join me at the pit. The money will be handy and we'll all benefit from the wage you'll be bringing home."

It had always been there, the darkness, waiting to engulf him. From his earliest childhood, he had been afraid of it. He supposed it stemmed from the claustrophobic terror of being locked in the small, dank cupboard under the stairs, the favourite punishment meted out by his brutish father. He remembered the first time he'd suffered, only three or perhaps four, when his father had lifted him and roughly thrown him into the darkness; he couldn't remember what for but he remembered the fear and horror of being unable to get out, the smell of damp and decay, not daring to cry aloud for fear his father would extend his time in there as further punishment. He'd learned very quickly to be a good boy but there was still the odd time he'd be locked in and he dreaded it. Eddie was braver than him. He didn't fear the darkness, nor was he claustrophobic. He was braver than his twin but he didn't ever once make him feel ashamed for his fear. Matthew could still recall the first time he'd whispered to Eddie, "Will you hold my hand? I'm afraid of the dark," and Eddie had taken his hand and whispered back, "Through the darkness," telling him it was OK, that there was nothing to be afraid of. Matthew was always comforted by that and grateful that his twin didn't judge his phobia and dismiss it as nonsense.

Few of us are unfortunate enough to experience the terror that gripped Matthew as hand in hand, he and Eddie followed their father into the black tunnel, leaving daylight behind for the darkness below. The lamps helped a little but Matthew was still shaking, though doing his level best to hide this from the beady eyes of his father, who glanced at them occasionally in the dim lamplight, before again lifting his pick axe to hack away at the mine wall. Month after month, rain, hail or shine, they trudged down the shaft into the pit below, relieved when their shift was over and they could emerge once more into the fresh air and head wearily home to wait their turn in the big tin bath in front of the fire. While Eddie adjusted and accepted his fate, Matthew never grew used to the horror of the darkness and at night he would dream of escaping the drudgery and fear of the mine. Quietly, while Eddie slept, he would reach out and place his hand in that of his sleeping brother and long for the day when he would never have to go there again.

Months turned into years and the boys grew into early manhood, Matthew's spirits and health declining in equal measure. He would always look forward with happy anticipation to the two days' holiday for Christmas and Boxing Day, a brief and welcome respite from the dreadful toil of the mine. Just before their nineteenth birthday and two weeks before the longed for holiday, he fell ill and within days was dead from some unknown infection, no less deadly for the lack of a name, Eddie holding his hand as always, as he slipped into eternal darkness, weeping quietly, his mother at his side, sobbing uncontrollably. In the days and weeks that followed, Eddie took some comfort in the passing of his beloved sibling by telling himself over and over that Matthew's wish had been granted; he was free of the mine and at peace. He would never need to fear the dark again.

The years passed and Eddie married, had children and continued his work in the mine. He'd never been afraid of the darkness nor had he thought of finding other work. This was his lot in life and he accepted it. The morning of 10 December 1902 was his and Matthew's twenty-sixth birthday. It had been snowing heavily for days but this didn't stop work at the mine and at five in the morning, just as he did every other day save for the Sabbath, Eddie ate a meagre breakfast, kissed his wife and children goodbye and set out for the colliery at the outskirts of the village. The mile and a half's walk was a melancholy one as he thought of his dead sibling and as he entered the shaft, he whispered, "Happy birthday," to his much-loved twin.

It was at about ten o'clock when they first heard the low rumbling sound, the pit horses becoming agitated as the noise grew louder and then the ceiling and walls around them crumbled and the screams of the men echoed around the chamber for a time before only the low moans of the dying could be heard.

Eddie lay curled on his side, crushed beneath the rock fall, unable to move and for the first time in his life he felt afraid of the dark. He thought of his family and the tears slipped silently down his cheeks as he lay there, alone and dying. His breathing was laboured and he knew his death was close at hand and he thought then of Matthew. He saw, in his mind's eye, the fearful face of his twin as his father loomed over him and another beating began. He heard the soft sobs of his brother, as he lay in the bed next to him, pretending to sleep so that Matthew wouldn't suffer further embarrassment and humiliation. He thought of the times he'd held his little hand in his own and offered the only comfort he could. He remembered the happy times when they'd played and laughed and dreamed of a life neither of them would ever know. He prayed silently for the end to come quickly, for his wife and children and for his mother who would lose another son. As the groans of his stricken colleagues fell silent and they succumbed one by one, he thought of all the wives and mothers whose lives were changed forever by the collapse of the shaft and an overwhelming sadness engulfed him. The sadness of waste and futility. The sadness of lives cut short by tragedy. The unfairness of it all. He felt cold and afraid and hoped his end would not be long in coming and as he struggled for air, he felt someone take his hand. He felt the firm grip that he knew so well and he knew instantly who it was and felt comforted and at peace.

Matthew took his brother's hand and squeezed gently and as he closed his eyes on the world for the last time, Eddie knew that his twin had come to take him home.

The Missing Patient

The coach and four left London promptly. It was going to be a long and tedious journey before we would arrive in York, scheduled for 23 December and as I took my seat, I studied my fellow passengers, hopeful that at least the company would be convivial. There were two more male passengers and two females; I assumed, rightly as it turned out, that they were two couples. We were to pick up another passenger en route and as the journey was a long one, we would be making several stops with two overnight stays at coaching inns, the first with the rather apt name of The Weary Traveller.

We introduced ourselves and I learned that I was travelling alongside two married couples, unrelated to each other but both travelling north to spend the Christmas season with their respective families. Mr and Mrs Harper were about to become grandparents; their daughter was due to be confined early in the new year. Mr and Mrs Jenkins were excited about seeing their brood of grandchildren in Newcastle and they would be travelling on from York. When it was my turn to explain my journey, I informed my companions that I was relocating permanently to take up practice as a general practitioner in York itself, beginning immediately after Christmas. I did not go into details but I will tell you now, that I was not long qualified and that this was to be my first position; I was excited and terrified in equal measure. I had no family to welcome me to my new home and truth to tell I was not really looking forward to Christmas, which would be spent in a small hotel as my cottage would not be ready until 3 January.

We settled down for the journey and wrapped in blankets against the chilly weather outside, the conversation was pleasant enough. I recall feeling a little sorry for the coachmen, sitting up on top in the teeth of the bitter wind and even spared a thought for the horses, while we inside the coach were as comfortable as could be, given the bumpy roads which caused the coach to lurch about, some of us almost losing our seats at times. My two male companions and I had had the foresight to bring hip flasks; mine was filled with brandy, the other two with scotch and this helped warm us through well enough, although both ladies politely decline the invitation. By the time, we reached our first stop, we had spent several hours becoming better acquainted and although somewhat shaken about and rather chilled, despite the travelling rugs and alcohol, we made a happy enough little group as we entered the rather charming, if small inn.

We found a corner by the blazing fire in the main room of the Inn and sat down to enjoy a hearty meal, joined later by the coachmen once they had seen to the horses. It was not a long stay, forty-five minutes later we were back on the road, by which time it had begun to rain. My sympathies for the coachmen and horses rose several notches and indeed the inside of the coach was not much warmer but at least it was dry.

By the time, we had left London long behind, the weather had turned from wind and rain to heavy snow. It was freezing and uncomfortable as the coach swayed to and fro, hour after hour and we were all of us, extremely relieved to arrive at The Weary Traveller; there were indeed seven very weary travellers and four tired horses, all in need of rest and sustenance. The inn was the largest of those we had stopped at on our journey; it was rather isolated but it looked spacious at least from the outside and there was the promise of more cheerful firesides and hearty, warming food waiting for us inside. The coachmen took the horses to be stabled while we made our way indoors.

The interior was quite charming, if rather rustic and I was indeed glad to see two very welcoming fires, one at either end of the large room into which we entered. The host welcomed us warmly and we were all shown to our rooms on the first floor before re-convening by the fireside to enjoy our evening meal. Conversation flowed freely as we discussed our future plans and speculated on our fellow traveller, who would be joining us the next day. The ale flowed freely, the meat and potato stew both smelled and tasted delicious and we were soon thawed out, the heat of the flames welcome and mesmerising. I felt I could quite happily sleep there in my chair, in front of that blazing fire, the smell of the burning wood was something I always enjoyed. Several pleasant hours had passed and several warming drinks had been consumed, (the ladies had retired earlier, both being exhausted from the journey) when the door was thrown open and a bedraggled looking young lad rushed in and stopped, gasping for breath. The icy blast of cold air which accompanied him and the white flakes of snow which had settled on his all too thin jacket, testament to the worsening weather outside. I jumped up, pushed the door shut against the wind and called to the landlord to fetch a brandy, as the lad was soaked to the skin. I guided him to the fire and sat him down beside my travelling companions. I judged him to be about fourteen or fifteen as he downed the brandy, shuddering at the taste, his young face screwed up as the warm liquid hit his throat; it had the desired affect however, as he was soon calmer and able to tell us that he had been sent from a local farm because his mistress was ill and needed help.

"Master says there may be horses here what can be sent to fetch a doctor," he explained, "we have no horses, only cows and sheep."

"Then you're in luck, young man," I replied, "I'm Dr Manning and I'll be glad to come and attend your mistress."

After enquiring how far away the farm was, I hastily donned the boots and waterproof coat loaned to me by the landlord and the two of us set out into the night. The weather had indeed worsened further since our arrival and several inches more snow now lay on the ground, added to which a heavy fog had descended, although mercifully, it had stopped snowing, for now at least. The air was crisp and icy against my cheeks and I felt heartily sorry for the lad, who had barely had time to dry out and whose clothing and footwear was totally inadequate for such foul weather. It was as well the lad knew his way, for it was difficult to see a hand in front of you, so dense was the fog; the light from the one lantern we had, all but useless. I was glad of the landlord's sturdy boots for I now determined the snow was at least four or five inches deep and it slowed us down considerably. It was freezing, the fog swirling all about us as I questioned the lad about the nature of his mistress's illness, I could tell from his reply that the poor mite was shivering uncontrollably and that he was struggling for breath in the teeth of the wind and at this point, I decided he was in more need of the great coat than I. The lady in question had suddenly taken ill at supper and had had to be carried to her bed; from his description I believed that she was delirious and quite possibly had a fever. I would be able to determine nothing further until I was able to examine her in person and besides, the weather made it both difficult to talk and to hear. Further conversation was pointless. I estimated it took us a good thirty-five minutes or so to reach the farm which was situated well back from the road; we had passed through an open gateway and walked another five minutes or more before I could make out a large farmhouse, welcome lighting coming from several windows on both the ground and the upper floors. Davy, for such was the lad's name, was quite exhausted from his endeavours and his master, a Mr William Allen, sent him straight to get dry, take a hot drink and a bite to eat and then to bed. The house was warm and welcoming and everywhere, there were obvious signs of the coming season; holly and other evergreens festooning the mantel piece in the kitchen through which we had entered, as well as over doorways and the large, oak dresser on the wall opposite the fireplace.

Mr Allen was clearly anxious about his wife and after introductions, he led me up the stairs to my patient who lay propped up on her pillows. She was clearly very unwell and simply by looking at her I judged her to be feverish; there was an unhealthy sheen to her face and she had a ruddy hue to her cheeks. The room was stiflingly hot so before I began my examination, I ordered Mr Allen to open the window a little, explaining that it was essential to cool down the room. I told him too, to allow the fire to die out; Mrs Allen would be more than warm enough thanks to the bed coverings. I could see he was unsure and about to protest but I explained why it was necessary, telling him he could light it again once her fever had abated and he complied without further comment.

After a thorough examination, I was happy that my patient was not in any real danger; I had asked Mr Allen for a wet cloth and had applied this to her brow. I instructed him to continue to do this as it would help make his wife more comfortable. I reassured him that the fever would pass and impressed upon him again that the room should be kept cool. I could see he was still anxious so I wrote out a prescription; it was only for a tonic but he would not know that and it did indeed seem to reassure him. He placed it on the table at his wife's bedside and gently took her hand as he kissed her forehead and brushed the damp hair from her brow.

He replaced the cloth and turning to me, said, "Thank-you, Doctor; I will send for the prescription first thing in the morning."

Mrs Allen was now sleeping more comfortably and the room had cooled considerably. Happy that I could do no more, I took my leave.

The weather had yet again taken a turn for the worse; it was snowing heavily once more, thick fluffy flakes were falling fast and it was a complete whiteout. It was virtually impossible to see my way forward and I struggled to find my way back to the road. It seemed to take forever to find my way back to the inn and for some time, I feared that I would lose the road and become hopelessly lost. I was wet through and exhausted by the time I staggered into the now deserted bar. I was glad to see the fire still blazing and the landlord waiting for me with a warming glass of brandy. I shrugged off my wet clothes and sat by the fire to warm myself as the landlord brought me a welcome bowl of broth, thick with vegetables along with another glass of brandy. He sat down opposite me with a glass of his own.

"How did you find your patient?" he enquired.

"Mrs Allen had a slight fever but she is not in any danger," I replied.

"Mrs Allen?"

He blanched.

"Mrs Allen? Are you quite sure?"

"Yes, at Hartside Farm, about two miles west of here," I told him.

"That can't be right," he told me, "Hartside Farm has been deserted for five years or more, Mr Allen left after his wife died; I had thought you were going to the Lawson's at Waverly."

I looked at his pale face and tried to make sense of what he had just said. The Allens had been real, I knew it. I had felt her pulse, touched her fevered brow. I had spoken to her husband and given him instructions. I had been in a warm and welcoming farmhouse. I told him as much but his face betrayed his bewilderment and disbelief.

"Mrs Allen died six years back," he said, "oddly enough it was about this time of year she first took ill. Initially, it seemed she'd recover. It was just before the new year she took a turn for the worse. Dead in days. Allen took it real bad; he did. Started neglecting the farm. About a year after, he sold off all his livestock and left for Cumberland. Had family there apparently. Always thought it a bit queer he never sold the house. Maybe intended coming back at some point. Who knows what goes through a man's head when he's grieving bad."

I found his tale hard to reconcile with what I'd seen and heard last night. The Allens I met were very much alive and well. I'd heard the sheep and the cattle in the barns, been greeted by a friendly sheepdog. I'd felt her pulse for God's sake. I'd spoken to them both. I'd felt the warmth of the farmhouse fires, smelt the wood smoke. More to the point, we had all seen and heard Davy. *How could I have imagined all that? It was impossible, nonsensical.*

"There has to be an explanation," I replied, "I'll go back tomorrow," I said and was both relieved and grateful when he said he would accompany me.

We arranged to be up early to make our journey as the coach was due to leave immediately after breakfast at nine o'clock, although I had my doubts we would be able to continue our journey; the snow was still falling thick and fast. It was already well past midnight but tired as I was, I could not sleep. I tossed and turned, reliving the evening's events. I recalled the journey to the farm with young Davy, the warmth of the farmhouse after the cold struggle through the snow. I replayed my conversation with Mr Allen and my examination of his wife. I could picture the farmer's relieved face as I told him his wife was not in any danger. None of it made any sense; there had to be a logical explanation. *How could Hartside Farm be empty, no family present? Where had I been and to whom had I been speaking?* The night dragged slowly on and I think I dozed briefly but I was glad when it was time to get up and go down to meet the landlord.

We set out in the direction I had taken last evening, both dressed against the weather which as I had suspected would delay our journey for today at least. It had stopped snowing but it lay, several feet deep now and the cold, frosty air bit sharply. It was difficult going and conversation was limited to a few, brief exclamations of dismay as one or other of us lost his footing and declared misery against the chill. I was relieved when eventually the farmhouse came into sight.

"There it is," I declared, pointing it out to my companion.

He looked at me and I could see his confusion.

"Yes, that's Hartside alright, but as I've said, no one lives there now," he informed me.

"Impossible," I replied but my stomach flipped and I was not certain of my own declaration.

It was deathly quiet, there were no sounds of sheep bleating, I could see no cattle. There was no warning bark from the friendly sheepdog. I told myself that they would all still be safely inside warm barns, out of the snow but I was beginning to feel very uneasy. I looked at my companion's face and knew that he too was feeling it. It was too quiet as we approached the house which now showed no outward signs of life; it looked sadly neglected now that I could see it in the early morning light, the weak winter sun just peeping over the horizon.

I knocked on the door and the sound echoed inside. My stomach flipped again and it was with a growing sense of horror that I tried the door; locked.

"I'm going around the back," I informed my companion and to my relief, he nodded his assent and we both made our way around the building.

It was becoming even clearer that the house was empty but I was determined to get inside. *Surely,* I thought, *I would find evidence of the family I had so recently attended. Perhaps Mrs Allen had taken a turn for the worse after all and Mr Allen had decided she needed to be transported to the nearest infirmary.* The absurdity of this idea considering the weather, I refused to countenance as I brushed aside the landlord's conviction that they had left five years ago.

The rear of the house looked even more derelict. Windows were broken and the back door was unlocked. I rushed into the kitchen and stopped in my tracks; it was empty. No welcoming fire blazed in the hearth. No cheerful holly and other Christmas decorations were to be seen. It smelled of damp and decay, the victim of several years of neglect. I turned to my companion and the look of bewilderment on his face in no way matched the sheer disbelief and terror that swept over me. I felt chilled to the bone. Turning on my heels I left the kitchen and ran up the stairs to the bedroom I had visited last evening; I heard my companion follow hot on my heels.

The door was slightly ajar but even as I pushed it open and crossed the threshold I knew it was, like the rest of the house, quite empty. I stood in disbelief and utter bewilderment, nausea washing over me; the bed and table were gone, the large wardrobe was gone, the window which had been opened last evening was grimy from years of neglect. The hearth was cold and bare. I stared in disbelief at the window, the hearth, the space where the bed and furniture ought to be. This made no sense and I struggled to stay calm, the thump of my heart beating in my chest painfully, the blood pounding in my ears.

Then I saw it. I stooped and picked it up, turned to my companion and handed it to him, watched as both confusion and fear spread over his face as he read what was written on the paper before he handed it back to me. I didn't need to read it; after all, I knew what was written there and what it was. My prescription…

Retribution

He hadn't meant to do it. It had been an accident. It was what he did next that changed an accident into something far more heinous, far more craven and unforgivable but there's an old saying isn't there? 'Be sure your sins shall find you out.'

The day had begun much like any other. He'd risen at six, showered, dressed, eaten breakfast – poached eggs on toast, drank the richly aromatic coffee, kissed his wife and left for work. He felt refreshed, having slept well. The case he was working on was shaping up to be a winner and his client was satisfied with the work he was doing on his behalf. Life was good. He would soon make a partnership at the prestigious law firm he worked for and then they would be able to start the family they both wanted. A bigger house, a new car, holidays on the cruise ships they both so enjoyed. It was all within reach and if he pulled off this case and his client walked free, it was all in the bag, his for the taking.

The weather was fine, cold but clear and looking back afterwards, he simply couldn't figure out what had gone wrong. The winding country lane was quiet enough, and as was often the case at that early hour of the day, he hadn't encountered another vehicle for almost two miles. The thump took him completely by surprise and it was in horror and disbelief that he watched something in his rear view mirror as it landed in the road, several hundred yards behind the car. The squeal of the brakes broke the silence of the hitherto peaceful morning and sent a flock of birds soaring into the skies. He sat for what seemed like minutes, his hands gripping the steering wheel, staring at the motionless lump in the rear view mirror.

Springing into action, he threw open the car door and ran to investigate the heap that he could now clearly see, was the body of a young male. Trembling, he knelt over the still body and tentatively turned it over. Horrified, he recoiled as lifeless blue eyes stared up at him. Forever afterwards, he could not explain what he did next. He stood, quickly looking about him for any signs of other human activity. Satisfied that he was alone, he took hold of the feet and dragged the corpse of his victim off the road and into the undergrowth of the trees lining the lane. Making sure the body was well hidden from the view of the road, he quickly covered it with twigs and crisp, dead leaves and then he sped back to his car and drove off at speed.

He wasn't sure how he got through the rest of the day. Meetings with colleagues and his client, preparing case notes, eating and drinking, trying to do all the normal, everyday things in a normal, everyday way. They were all a blur and when it was finally time to go home, having toyed with taking the longer, motorway route, in the end he couldn't resist retracing the morning's journey. He had to see if anything was amiss, if the body had been discovered, if the lane was swarming with police and incident vehicles.

He could tell that all was quiet on the lane and in the gloomy darkness of the autumnal night, only his headlamps lighting the way, he approached and drove slowly past the scene of the morning's accident with relief and a growing sense of guilt. He wondered briefly how long it would be before all hell broke loose and someone missed the young lad whose life he had snuffed out in an instant and an investigation would get under way. Why hadn't he simply reported it? It had, after all been an accident. The youth had appeared from nowhere and it had all happened in the blink of an eye, it really wasn't his fault. He'd reasoned that the police might have thought he was speeding (he was but could they have proven it?). They would have breathalysed him (he'd had several drinks the previous evening but he didn't think he'd be over the limit). He thought it might play badly with the senior partners. Over and over, he played it all through the journey home and decided he'd done the right thing. His career was just taking off; he couldn't afford any hiccups that would leave a black mark against his name. He knew he was being utterly selfish, callous even but he brushed these emotions aside and his mind was made up. He would do and say nothing. It would be as if it had never happened.

Nevertheless, he slept badly that night, his sleep disturbed by thoughts of the accident. He couldn't erase the sight of those staring, dead eyes looking up at him, accusing, the awful thud as he'd hit the lad, the sight of him hitting the ground in his rear view mirror. Finally, at 3 a.m., he got up, leaving his sleeping wife and went downstairs to make himself a drink. Taking it to his study, he switched on his laptop and began searching the online news threads. Nothing. No reports of a missing teenager, no reports of a hit and run death or the discovery of a body. Relieved, he was about to shut down when he saw it, briefly, little more than a flash before it was gone; the bruised and battered face of his victim and those eyes, piercing and accusatory. The breath left his body, the blood pounded in his head, his heart thumped painfully in his chest but he found himself staring at his desktop apps and nothing more. He slammed the lid closed and staggered back to the kitchen. He needed something stronger than tea. He poured himself a large glass of scotch and hand shaking, he sat down at the farmhouse style table and buried his head in his hands. He was still there the next morning when his wife came down to make breakfast. He'd managed to convince Sarah that he'd just been unable to sleep, pressure at work, thoughts running wild. He hadn't wanted to disturb her, he'd explained. He wasn't sure how long it had been before he fell asleep but the three, large glasses of scotch had surely helped and his sleep had then been deep and dreamless.

He knew that this morning he would definitely be over the limit and so he kept his speed down, anxiously glancing in his mirrors for any signs of a police car on his tail. Despite his high state of agitation, he couldn't resist the compulsion, the absolute urge to once more drive past the scene of the crime, stopping at the exact spot where it had happened, only the day before. *God,* he thought now, *just a day, is that all? It feels like an eternity.* It was as he was pulling away that he saw him, in the mirror, the lad who should be lying in the corpse, under the dead leaves; he was staring at him, his hand outstretched, a finger pointing directly at him. His blood ran cold and he hit the brakes, jolting forward against the seat belt. When he looked again, there was the only the empty lane, stretching out behind him.

"Guilt," he said aloud, "it's just my guilty conscience. I need to get a grip, I need to stay calm, sort stuff, starting with the car."

Flicking through the contact list on the dash monitor, he tapped connect and as the dial tone broke the silence, he accelerated and pulled away. Several minutes later he had booked his car into the garage to have the number plate replaced and the bumper checked. His initial check for damage had revealed some minor scuff marks and scratches to the bumper but the number plate was badly dented and would need to be replaced. He was surprised that there hadn't been more damage given the impact but perhaps he just couldn't see it. The main problem now was how he would explain any questions as to how the damage had arisen in the first place. He would give it some thought but best to keep it simple he thought. Perhaps he could say he'd hit a stray sheep, that would work wouldn't it?

In the end, it proved much easier than he'd anticipated. No one at the garage questioned him and Sarah hadn't seen the car, either immediately after the accident as it was already dark when he'd returned home that night, or after its brief sojourn in the workshop. He felt rather pleased with himself, congratulating himself on his good luck, only briefly now feeling a tinge of guilt and shame that he should be so uncaring, so blasé about it all. It was early days of course but as the days went by with no untoward activity on the lane or reports of a missing person in the news, he was beginning to feel he was going to get away with it and he couldn't help but feel relieved at his good fortune.

His life was going on pretty much as normal except for his conscience playing tricks on him. His nights were sleepless and he kept seeing him; he saw him at home in the house, he saw him in the lane and he saw him at work. What was worse, the visions (initially, he refused to think of them as anything else), began to be accompanied by a strong, offensive odour. He didn't recognise it at first, of course, the smell of corruption and decay; that would come later. That was when he finally acknowledged that the visions were real, that it wasn't just a guilty conscience, that he was being haunted. He began to dread the nights when he knew he would have to crawl into bed beside Sarah because he knew that if he managed to fall asleep, he would wake in the velvety black darkness of 2 a.m. drenched in sweat, the duvet thrown back in an effort to cool his overheated body. He would toss and turn for hours, 3 a.m., 4 a.m., tormented by what he'd done and the consequences of his behaviour afterwards.

Sarah would wake and try to comfort him, not really sure what it was he needed comfort for. He continued the lie about pressure of work but she was beginning to wonder if it was something else and began pressing him. He wondered, briefly if he should simply tell her the truth, the whole sordid, terrible truth but he balked at the idea. He believed she would never understand, that she would hate him, end their marriage and leave in disgust. He even thought she would call the police. Would she? She might. He couldn't risk it. He couldn't risk losing her but more than that, he couldn't risk her informing on him.

It was several weeks after the event that he plucked up the courage to venture into the corpse. He felt drawn to the spot where he'd hidden the body, as if he needed to reassure himself it was still there, that it wasn't walking about at night to torment him. As he approached the mound of leaves and twigs he saw to his horror that it was moving. For a heart stopping moment, he imagined his victim was about to get up and confront him but then he realised it was thousands of writhing maggots and other insects. It was then that the stench of rotting flesh assailed his nostrils and he recognised the odour that accompanied the nightly visitations. It was then that his world began imploding and he began the long descent into madness.

The nights continued to be an utter torment that was becoming unbearable and his days were falling apart, his work suffering as a result. He was so exhausted that as usual, he'd manage to fall asleep but then he'd be jolted awake and he would know that he was not alone, that he had come again. The nights were worse than the days. He could just about cope in the daylight but in the inky blackness of the night, his fears were magnified a hundred fold and the terror he felt reduced him to a quivering wreck. He would see him at the foot of the bed, staring with those icy eyes, or in a mirror, staring at him through the glass. He would see him in the garden, looking in on his life. There was no escape, for he was everywhere. Sarah's worries increased and she no longer believed it was just pressure of work. They argued, tension flaring and their marriage put under strain for the first time in five years. He began to believe she might really leave him now, distraught at the thought.

Then the inevitable happened. The head of chambers called him into his office and told him he was no longer required to work on the case, that the client had requested another barrister, one who was up to the job. Worse, if he didn't pull himself together, he would be asked to leave chambers altogether. This was the wake-up call he'd needed. He decided he had to pull himself together. He couldn't allow his life to fall apart for the sake of one error of judgment. His marriage, his career and his life were all at stake. He'd called at a pharmacy and bought an over the counter sleep aid; a good night's sleep was all he needed. Exhaustion was the problem and he had to sort it out and take back his life, get back to normal and put it all behind him, once and for all. That night he took one more pill than the stated dose and he slept, undisturbed for the first time in weeks. He repeated this over the next week with the same results and to his delight, the nightly visits stopped. He saw nothing of him on the way to work or in the office either. Life began to pick up its normal rhythm and he and Sarah began making plans for Christmas, their arguments forgotten, their marriage back on track. They would spend it at home before jetting off on Boxing Day for some well-deserved winter sunshine.

Christmas Eve was to be his last day at work for two weeks and he was looking forward to the break. The weather had taken a turn for the worse and for the last week, overnight temperatures had fallen well below zero, the daytime ones barely managing a degree or two above. The ground was permanently covered in a hard hoar frost so that despite the lack of snow, the world took on the magical look of a Christmas card. The gritters were on almost permanent deployment but the main roads remained passable so he chose to drive his usual route, always driving at a sensible speed, always careful and alert and so it was this morning, 24 December, a bright, bitterly cold day, that he set out as usual and followed his well-known routine. He was whistling along to a tune on the radio, careful to stay watchful but enjoying the winter wonderland countryside as he drew close to that scene, the scene that no longer tormented him, the scene that was now just like any other en route. The scene that he'd managed to erase so successfully from his conscience. It was as if it had never happened. It was as he turned the bend that he saw the figure in the road and this time managed to swerve to avoid it. As he did so, he hit a patch of black ice, the car spinning wildly out of control, all the advice about what to do in this situation, deserting him. To his horror, his foot appeared stuck to the accelerator as he scrabbled desperately to regain control of the wheel and then, just before the car left the road and hit the tree, he saw it, him one last time.

In the split second before impact, the thought occurred to him that they'd find him now, the young lad whose life he'd snuffed out and left so callously, so shamefully in a shallow grave. This was retribution; 'I deserve this.' They were smiling, those icy eyes, those long dead eyes, smiling as the car smashed into the tree trunk and his own eyes closed for ever.

At the Foot of the Stairs

The letter had arrived on Ian Garfield's desk on the cold, sunny morning of 26 September; its postmark proclaimed that its origin was India. Its instructions were clear and to the point; the author, one Jonathan Miller, required a house to rent. It must be in a quiet village, away from London but within comfortable travelling distance and fully furnished. There were to be no servant's resident, although a cook and a cleaner were required who would need to live nearby, the cook being required daily, the cleaner at least twice weekly and Miller himself suggested that these two roles may be suited to one person. There were a few further instructions regarding size, number of rooms and the optimum rent he was prepared to pay and an estimated arrival date, 30 October, a little over a month from the day of the letter's own arrival. He spent little time musing about his new client or his very precise instructions. A client's business was their own and Garfield was ever the professional.

Ian Garfield was a practical, well organised man and it took him less than a week to secure his client a house. Miller was already en route from India and would be arriving imminently. The house was situated in the village of Lynmead, about four miles south of Hemel Hempstead in

Hertfordshire and was pleasantly appointed. There were two reception rooms, a central hallway with a staircase leading to the only other floor, and to the rear of the ground floor, a decent sized, well equipped kitchen. The two bedrooms were both of a good size, with double beds, though it being an older house, of Victorian origin, there were no ensuite bathrooms. The one bathroom it did have, was at least a decent one with the luxury of a shower cubicle. Garfield was sure his client would approve, particularly as the rent was reasonable and he had managed to secure the services of a middle-aged lady, by the name of Mrs Parkinson, who would both clean and cook for the agreed wage.

All was ready well in advance of Miller's arrival, who had requested that Garfield meet him in the local pub in Lynmead, rather than at his offices in London; Miller did not wish to be delayed by the inconvenience of first having to travel to the capital to sign papers and pick up keys. Garfield was not averse to this request and so on the due date, he found himself sitting by the fire of the saloon bar of The Fox Cub in Lynmead. The keys to Yew Cottage and the papers to be signed were in the briefcase at his feet. The pub was a pleasant one, with only a few customers for it was early afternoon and Garfield at last found himself wondering about the client he had never met. He had been musing on this subject for some time, when a draft of cold air announced a new arrival. He looked up to see a tall, striking man, well dressed in a dark navy, double breasted overcoat and wearing a fedora hat, quietly close the door and look about him. As he was carrying a small suitcase, Garfield surmised that this was the mysterious client; he raised his hand in greeting and stood as the stranger approached. The handshake was firm and the voice, deep and strong.

"Good afternoon, Garfield, pleased to meet you."

Garfield returned the greeting and having established his client was a whisky drinker made his way to the bar. There was a little small talk; Garfield hoped the journey had been a pleasant one, the weather was mild for the time of year but the formalities were concluded in short order and Miller drained his glass; he had no wish to linger over pleasantries in The Fox Cub. Neither did he require that Garfield accompany him to the cottage; he simply requested directions and having established that Mrs Parkinson would be present to cook an evening meal, the two men shook hands once more and parted company.

Miller easily found the house and quickly understood why it was named a cottage, although he could see no yew trees anywhere nearby. Perhaps in the back garden, he pondered. The cottage was situated at the far end of the village, away from the pub, the village green and the only shop. It was not large, but then as a single man, he did not require it to be so, however he found its interior warm and to his liking. The furnishings were comfortable and unostentatious. The sitting room looked out over the rear garden but he could still find no obvious signs of the yews from which the cottage took its name. Beyond the garden, which was not large, he could see there was a churchyard. He chose the rear bedroom which overlooked the cemetery and the rather pretty church, as he liked the view from the window, from where he could now see the cottage took its name; yew trees, the tree of graveyards and symbol of death. The thought of this bothered him not a jot.

Mrs Parkinson had prepared a hearty beef stew with dumplings and the delicious aroma reminded Miller of just how hungry he was, calling him back downstairs to eat. Mrs Parkinson duly served her new employer his meal and departed after agreeing to return at eight the next morning to prepare his breakfast.

His first night passed quietly enough and he woke the next morning, refreshed and hungry. After his breakfast of bacon and eggs, washed down with piping hot coffee, he set about finishing his unpacking. He had not much in the way of belongings, although a trunk was due to arrive within a day or two. Storing his suitcase on top of the large, double wardrobe, he picked up the small, velvet pouch he had placed on his bed. From it, he withdrew a magnificent, blood red ruby and holding it up to the daylight at the window, he examined it hungrily. He stood, admiring it for several minutes before carefully replacing it in the pouch. He had not yet decided what he was going to do with his ill-gotten gains; the ruby was not his, or at least it had not been until he had stolen it from its place in the temple at Jaipur.

The theft had been accomplished easily enough; indeed, he had been utterly surprised at the ease of his success and he had fled the country afterwards without any problems but after all, he had done it many times before. He had not been deterred at all by stories of curses and warnings about the ruby; he was not a superstitious man, he did not believe in the supernatural, nor was he a religious man so the theft of a gem from a religious artefact in the heart of a Hindu temple bothered him not at all: his conscience, if he'd ever had one, was untroubled; it was just another theft and he had executed more than his fair share of those; he'd kept his eye on the end game and now, here he was, safely back in England, with a new name and all the time in the world to decide how he would liquidate his prize.

Several days went by without incident and he began to settle into his new home, his new life and his new name. He kept himself to himself; he shunned the company at The Fox Cub, preferring to take a whisky or two in the solitude and comfort of his own fireside. Indeed, in the days that followed his arrival, his only exchange of words with any other human being, was with Mrs Parkinson, so when the vicar called at the end of his first week, to welcome him to the village and to enquire whether he would attend the little church of St Dismas of the Cross, Miller had politely made it clear that it would not be the case.

The cottage was cosy enough and with one or two of his own belongings here and there, his own books on the shelf by the hearth and his own shaving brush and razor in the bathroom, he felt very much at home. He fell into a routine that altered very little as the weeks went by. He would rise, take breakfast, read the papers, take a walk, usually managing to avoid villagers, passing the time of day if he did but not stopping to get better acquainted. His evenings were spent with a good book in front of a roaring fire, with several glasses of whisky before bed.

He grew used to the noises the cottage made as it settled down for the night, so he was understandably startled, when one night at the end of the second week in December he was rudely awoken by a loud noise which he thought came from the staircase. He lay stock still for several moments fearing an intruder but there was no repeat of the sound and so he got out of bed to investigate. Able to see easily enough without the benefit of switching on the light, he went to the top of the stairs, where he stood peering down to the bottom. For a fleeting moment, he thought he saw something lying at the foot of the stairs but switching on the landing light, all was as it should be. He thought something may have fallen over but nothing appeared disturbed anywhere and reassured he returned to his bed just as the church clock struck one, was soon asleep once more and spent the rest of the night undisturbed.

Next morning, it being a bright, dry day he decided to go for his usual stroll after breakfast and turned towards the churchyard. Although an atheist, he was able to enjoy the fine architecture of sacred buildings and while the church was certainly not grand, it was nevertheless pleasing to the eye. He stopped to admire the stained glass windows above the solid oak doors, the clock tower and clock itself. He sat for a time on a bench beneath a yew, near the gate and enjoyed the fresh air and quiet solitude, the silence punctuated now and then by birdsong, before returning to the cottage. The choice of Lynmead had been a good one. He liked it here.

Mrs Parkinson was busy cleaning upstairs so he made himself a coffee and took his newspaper to the sitting room. The theft from the temple in India had excited little interest here, an article in The Times, which Garfield had been instructed to send every week. The local newspaper mentioned nothing. Eagerly, in the early days, he had scanned the pages for any news which might cause alarm but found none and reassured yet again that he was safe, he sat by the fire making plans in his head. He had already decided to lay low in Lynmead until the spring and when his six months' lease expired he planned to sail to America; once there, he would decide how to sell the ruby.

By the time, he retired to bed that evening, the weather had taken a turn for the worse; it was raining hard and a gale was blowing; however, he was tired enough to soon fall into a deep sleep, oblivious to the howling wind and the rain lashing his windowpane. He had been asleep for several hours when he was awoken by a loud thump, thump, thump in rapid succession, again, he thought coming from the stairs. He rushed onto the landing and peered down to the foot of the stairs; there at the bottom he was sure he could see the outline of a large, dark shape. Startled, he switched on the light and was both relieved and bewildered to see nothing there. Perhaps, he thought, it was the wind, for the gale was still howling and the rain pelting the doors and windows; perhaps it was merely shadows created by an over active imagination, although ordinarily, he would have scoffed at this.

Rattled, despite himself, he returned to bed and lay listening to the storm raging outside his bedroom window. The church clock struck one as he tried to rationalise what he had just heard and seen. Shadows, the storm and his imagination, he decided. He was not a man easily scared but even he liked to have certainty as much as possible and in being unable to determine the real cause of the strange noise, he had to admit to feeling a little shaken. He did not know how long he lay awake but he was certainly asleep again before the clock struck the half hour after two; he had clearly heard the two chimes on the hour. He slept undisturbed until just after seven when he awoke with a blinding headache.

In the cold light of day, he dismissed his concerns; everything seemed normal but he nevertheless searched the hall closely. He tested each stair for squeaks, which he found on one or two but he admitted to himself that these in no way accounted for the odd noises of the night. There seemed to be nothing amiss and nothing that could be the cause of the nightly disturbances. Once again, he dismissed it all as the storm, which had now abated, leaving a calm, though cloudy day.

Refusing breakfast, he instead decided to take a walk in the hope of clearing his head. Preferring to avoid the village and its occupants, he once again turned towards the church. He enjoyed looking at the headstones and reading the inscriptions and he liked the quiet calmness he found there among the dead; no one to bother him and ask awkward questions. Today, he thought he might take a look inside the church, if it was open, just for curiosity's sake.

He was in luck, it was indeed unlocked, as small country churches often are and he made his way into the rather dark and gloomy interior; as the day was cloudy, little daylight entered through the stained glass. He stood quietly for a few moments until he became accustomed to the gloom and then he made his way up the central aisle towards the altar. It was not remarkable, he thought although he did acknowledge the statuary as being rather well done. He looked about, chuckling to himself as he noted there was nothing here to interest the thief in him; this was no gilded, foreign temple with glittering jewels to tempt him. It was all rather plain and understated and the irony of the name chosen for this little, country church made him laugh, although just for a moment, he thought perhaps he should send the ruby back.

"Nonsense," he chided himself. "It's worth thousands. Why would I give it up now after all I've been through to get it?"

Back in the warmth of the cottage, he took it from its pouch and held it up to the light. He could see St Dismas in the distance and once more, thought about posting the gem back but it was a fleeting thought, his innate greed getting the upper hand. He'd got away with it and the prize was his to keep.

Despite his bravado, his nights were now following a familiar pattern and each successive night, the noise of thumping on the stairs grew louder. The shape he thought he saw at the foot of the stairs also grew in form and size and alarmingly began to take on the shape of a human body, lying crumpled in the gloom. Worse, he was now also troubled by bad dreams. Terrified, he would wake, sweating in a tangle of bed sheets, from each recurring nightmare and recall in horror that he had fallen down the stairs, to lie in a broken heap at the bottom. With each passing night, the detail increased; he could feel each bump as he tumbled from the top to the bottom. He could see himself lying still and either dead or dying at the foot of the stairs and then finally, in one hand, he saw that he was clutching the ruby, blood red in his hand.

Desperately tired from the successive nights of disturbed sleep and severely rattled by the nightly disturbances, he began to both look and feel ill. Mrs Parkinson could hardly fail to notice and worried, suggested he consult the local doctor.

"I'm sure a good tonic will help you sleep," she said, concern evident in her tone. "Doctor Mason will have something to suit."

He dismissed the idea, telling her, not unkindly that it was merely a cold and he would soon get over it; he knew the cause of his ailment and for the first time since he was a child, acknowledged that his conscience was troubling him. Guilt or was it fear? Once more, he briefly considered returning the ruby to its rightful place but the thought did not last long before he shrugged the thought aside once more and resolved to go to America; he did however, decide to bring his journey forward and now determined on leaving at the end of January; he would happily forfeit the remaining two months' rent. Accordingly, he began making plans and the thought of his coming adventure bolstered him somewhat and he rallied a little.

Only as night returned and each bedtime approached, did he begin once more, to feel uncomfortable. He had by now, begun to dread the nightly terrors, the noises from the stairs and the dreams. Common sense and his usual, practical manner told him it was all in his mind, a guilty conscience, nothing more but when he woke, bathed in sweat after yet another nightmare, his common sense deserted him and the fear increased. The dreams had become far more vivid and detailed; they always ended with him looking down on himself at the foot of the stairs, quite clearly dead and always he could also see the stolen ruby, now resembling a little pool of blood, clutched in his lifeless hand.

Christmas was fast approaching but he had no enthusiasm, no energy and no desire to celebrate the season. In any case, he knew no one as he had deliberately avoided making friends and his only regular companion was Mrs Parkinson. They had agreed that she would work as usual on Christmas Eve and then have Christmas Day off, returning on Boxing Day; she would leave him with cold cuts and ensure his larder was well stocked and he had readily agreed, indeed he was looking forward to some time alone. He intended to spend the day quietly, finalising his travel plans and perhaps going for a walk in the afternoon if the weather held.

Christmas Eve dawned and the weather, while cold, was at least dry. After yet another disturbed night (it was now his expectation that he would have nightly disturbances), he was tired and irritable. He wanted nothing more than for Mrs Parkinson to finish her chores and leave so mid-afternoon, when she had informed him that his food for the following day was all prepared, he told her to take the rest of the day off; surprised but pleased, she bade him, 'Merry Christmas,' and left before he could change his mind and insist she scrub the floors or wash the windows.

He spent the rest of the day and evening quietly sitting by the fire reading, a glass of his favourite whisky in hand, enjoying the familiar aroma and the warmth of the honey coloured liquid as it slid down his throat while he poured over maps of the USA, planning his trip. He still had not decided on his final destination or of how he would dispose of the ruby once there; he wanted only to be rid of it now. His rational self, told him it was nonsense but another nagging voice in his head told him it was cursed and that his dreams would only cease when it was no longer in his possession. He could not believe the change that had overcome him in the weeks he had been in Lynmead. He had gone from being a sane, cold, rational man to one who now believed he was cursed.

For hours, he remained by the fire, brooding on what he had done and not for the first time in recent days, he regretted having stolen the gem. He tussled with himself, wondering once again, whether he should attempt to return it but again his greed won through, despite his current fears. He would go to America and sell the damned thing and all would be well. He poured himself another glass of whisky (he had stopped counting after the fourth), and welcomed the comforting warmth spreading through him; he intended to be very drunk before going to bed.

It was well past eleven when he mounted the stairs to his bedroom and he was indeed unsteady on his feet. He glanced briefly out at the eerie darkness, noting a heavy fog had descended; he could not even make out the garden, let alone the graveyard beyond. Shivering, he pulled the curtains shut and made ready for bed. Exhausted and longing for sleep, yet also dreading the dreams he knew would come, he determined to stay awake long past the usual hour of his torment. He fetched the ruby from its hiding place and removed it from its little velvet pouch. Climbing into bed he picked up his book, turning the gem over and over in his hand before carefully replacing it in the pouch, unable to bear looking at it any longer. The clock struck midnight; one more hour and it might be safe to sleep. He did not hear the clock strike the half hour.

Mrs Parkinson found him at the foot of the stairs on Boxing Day. He was quite cold and the doctor said he had been dead for some time. His neck was broken but it was his face which caused them both the greatest shock for it was contorted, his mouth gaping in a silent scream, his eyes wide open and both agreed he looked terrified. In his stiff, cold hand lay a small, black velvet pouch; it was quite empty.

The House at The Top Of the Cliff

Emma had fallen in love with the house the moment she had first set eyes on it. The charming double fronted, Georgian facade, the large, mullioned windows that she knew would flood the rooms beyond with light, the large, well kept, wrap around gardens but most of all, the view out to sea which she just knew, would be unparalleled. She even loved the name, laughing at the mundane, unoriginal choice of 'Sea View'. The previous owners obviously lacked imagination in her humble opinion.

The interior had not disappointed either. The three large reception rooms on the ground floor were indeed light and airy and the modern, recently updated kitchen offered plenty of storage and workspace and had the advantage of bi-folding doors which looked out over the patio and gardens beyond. She loved the space it afforded, both in and outdoors and she knew she would be at home here, would never want to leave. She just hoped Matt would feel the same.

The master bedroom enjoyed the advantage of an ensuite bathroom, good sized and well appointed. There was a balcony where they could enjoy eating breakfast when the weather allowed. The room was large enough for their king sized bed and there was plenty of built in wardrobe space, not that Emma was one of those women who over indulged in unnecessary items of expensive clothing. The smallest of the three bedrooms, still a good sized double would act as her study. It too looked out over the cliff top to the sea and she knew she would find it restful and conducive to her work as a freelance copywriter.

"We have to have this house, Matt, it's perfect," she had said as they finished their viewing.

Matt had taken little persuading and had in fact been quite open to the idea and a second viewing had decided the matter. Their own smaller house in a neighbouring town was already sold and they'd moved in two months later. For Emma at least, the house meant the achievement of a dream. She'd always wanted a house by the sea but to find this gem, atop a cliff with such amazing views, spacious airy rooms and large well-tended garden, was her dream come true. The gardener was to be kept on and a cleaner engaged who would come each Friday. Emma liked a clean, tidy house but she had no intention of cleaning such a large house herself. Matt was and never would be a gardener, so the matter was settled and the staff employed.

Within weeks of moving in, it was clear Matt liked the house as much as Emma and he had managed to make the move without any negative impact on his business as a self-employed electrician. As she had known she would, Emma found her work space a haven of peace in which she enjoyed hours of undisturbed time to get through her busy schedule.

The summer after they moved in was a good one; long days of hot sunshine during which they enjoyed breakfast on the balcony, overlooking the sea, the weekend lunches on the patio, the evening suppers too, while the weather held. They would enjoy the long descent down the stone steps to the beach, enjoying the tang of the fresh, salty air, the icy cold sea water on their bare feet as they strolled along the water's edge. When the weather was less agreeable, which was not often that first summer, they would retreat indoors and sit at their kitchen table, drinking wine and making small talk, the kind of meaningless chatter that couples indulge in after years of marriage. Emma had known when she married Matt that he didn't want children. She was fine with that because back then, neither had she but now, a year after they'd moved in and were fully settled into life in what she believed would be their forever home, she began to brood, telling herself that a house of this size was a family home, that it needed the sound of children's laughter filling the rooms. She would stare longingly at babies in their prams and look with envy at the smiling faces of mothers as they cooed at their infants. Her clock was ticking and she was all too aware that it was now or never; she was also too well aware that convincing Matt would not be easy.

Their relationship had always been tempestuous, both of them stubborn and hot tempered. The arguments had always been loud and volatile but in the early years of their marriage, their making up had been every bit as passionate. They would argue over just about anything at all but more often than not, it was about money. He resented the fact that in the very early days, she was making much more than he was and more than once, she had accused him of being jealous of her higher income. In truth, he was more than a little resentful but as his own business took off, this feeling of envy receded somewhat. He still didn't earn as much as she did but he was making enough for the difference to no longer matter quite so much. His male ego was no longer quite so challenged.

Now, after seven years of marriage, they'd weathered the storms, although their making up was no longer the fun, passion fuelled lovemaking they'd once enjoyed. Sex had become much less frequent and now, after an argument, they would sulk for days, each one refusing to back down or be the first to say 'sorry'. Even so, she felt their marriage was a strong one and would survive so she made up her mind that she would tell Matt she wanted a baby. She hadn't really got as far as thinking what she'd do if, as she suspected would be the case, Matt's stance remained unchanged. How would that impact their marriage? So consumed was she by her desire to be a mother, she blindly refused to see the obvious cracks in her plan.

She was careful about how she broached it with him, knowing that he was unlikely to have changed his mind and that his temper could explode in a split second. She prepared his favourite meal, beef bourguignon, the delicious aroma filling the kitchen and making her feel hungry, despite the butterflies in her stomach at the thought of the conversation she was about to have with Matt. She had several bottles of his favourite Australian Shiraz to mellow his mood and she had taken care to look her best, without going over the top, which would surely raise his suspicions.

After a pleasant meal and a bottle and a half of the red wine, Emma felt that Matt was definitely relaxed and in a good mood so she decided it was now or never.

"I met a lovely woman today," she began.

"I think we're going to be friends. She has six month old twins."

She went on, looking at him to gauge his reaction. Matt's face remained sanguine and he nodded as if to say, 'OK,' so she was encouraged to plough on.

"They're boys and so cute. I got to thinking what it would be like if we had a baby. A boy maybe, for you to play footie with in the garden or a little girl I could teach to cook and bake."

She knew this sounded rather lame but even so, his tone made her jump, her skin prickle.

"No," Matt said emphatically, his face not changing but his tone leaving no doubt in her mind that he was very angry.

He slammed his hand on the table, making the crockery rattle and upsetting his glass of wine.

"I don't want children, never have, never will and this conversation is over. You knew that when you married me and you said you felt the same. What the fuck are you thinking? Don't ever mention this to me again," he said as he stood up abruptly and left the room.

She knew him well enough not to press the issue too soon but despite his warning not to bring up the issue of children again she was equally determined not to let it drop. When she did, a week or so later, the ensuing argument had been loud and vicious. Matt had furiously swiped his plate off the table, smashing it and his wine glass on the tiled floor, before storming out to the pub, leaving her to clear up his mess.

The tension between them only increased over the coming days and Emma acknowledged what she had really known all along; Matt would never back down, so she did the unthinkable. Every morning, she would simply flush her pill down the toilet, leaving the pack in the bathroom cabinet where it had always been. She knew Matt would be checking it and she was careful enough not to be too enthusiastic about sex. He had to believe she had given up on her decision to get pregnant so she was careful not to change their usual pattern of lovemaking. She was very careful too about monitoring the optimum time for love making. Nothing must appear out of the ordinary; she would appear to be content with what she had. She was careful to let him think he was the one initiating sex, just as always. Matt showed no signs of being suspicious that anything had changed. They'd been married for over seven years, the first flush of passion had long since waned and he had long since accepted that sex was now much less often than he would have liked. For her part, she would often find herself asking why it was that the things she had once loved so completely about him, were the very things she now hated, why the little foibles she'd once found so charming, now thoroughly irritated her. She wondered if he felt the same but not once did she question her decision to have a baby with a man she now clearly no longer loved or respected nor did she feel as guilty as she should have done about the way she'd gone about it. The madness she had engaged in completely escaped her.

To the outside world, theirs was a happy marriage. They appeared to have it all, successful at work, the large house, nice cars. No one would have guessed that inside the house on the top of the cliff, all was not as it appeared, that Emma was now playing a part, with Matt unwittingly playing along because, well, he had a man's needs and any port in a storm would do.

For several months, the deception with the pill appeared to be working. The prospect of a baby was never mentioned openly again but Emma's desire for motherhood had become an obsession and as each month passed and her body let her down, she would sit, staring out to sea, watching the waves roll onto the beach and shed silent tears of despair. Only when Matt came home did she paint on her smile and appear perfectly content. It was an Oscar winning performance.

They'd been in the house almost eighteen months when at last she realised with a thrill of excited anticipation that her period was late. She hardly dared to believe it could be true but the blue lines in the little window confirmed that she was pregnant. She sat staring at those two blue lines for what seemed like minutes before she carefully wrapped up the test and the packaging and put everything very carefully in the bottom of the waste bin outside. Only now, did the reality of what she'd done hit her. Matt she knew, would be furious and she realised she was dreading his reaction. Panicked, she decided to keep it to herself for as long as possible; she knew it couldn't be for long. Would he notice the absence of any sanitary products? She would have to continue to buy and pretend to use them. The charade with the pill would have to continue too. He mustn't guess until she was ready to tell him.

She hadn't taken into account the morning sickness that would ravage her each day. This she couldn't hide from him. At first, she'd said she must have a bug but this explanation could only hold good for a few days.

Matt predictably, was furious when finally, one morning, after he'd listened to her vomiting yet again, he roughly grabbed her arm and with his face only inches from hers said, "You're pregnant, aren't you?"

It was a statement rather than a question. He already knew the answer.

"My pill must have failed," she said feebly, barely able to look at him, "it happens sometimes. They're not a hundred percent effective."

"Well, you'll just have to get rid of it," he said, "we're not having this baby. Mistake or not, there'll be no baby in this house."

Indignant, Emma stood her ground.

"I'm not having an abortion," she told him, "If you don't want it, then I'll have this baby on my own. I'm more than capable of bringing up a baby alone if I have to." Matt had stormed out, slamming doors behind him and in the days that followed, their arguments grew ever more vicious, Matt spending more and more time in the pub and sleeping in the spare room. The cracks in their marriage that had been so evident, now split wide open and within a few short weeks they had reached the point of no return. 'Was this how all marriages unravelled?' she asked herself. 'How did things spiral out of control so quickly?' She didn't want to admit her own part in the disintegration of their relationship or the duplicity of her behaviour. All she really knew for certain was that they couldn't go on like this. It was over and they both needed to accept it and move on. Emma told Matt she wanted him to move out and that she wanted a divorce. Furiously, Matt told her he would never give her the house. It would have to be sold and they would split the proceeds. For her part, Emma was adamant that she would never leave the house and told him she'd fight with every fibre of her being to hold on to it.

"It was me who fell in love with this house," she told him, "it was me who wanted it so badly, me who made it into the home it is now. I've poured my heart and soul into this house and I'll never leave it!"

"And that is why I'll fight tooth and nail to make sure you don't keep it."

Matt spat viciously at her before storming out yet again. He moved into a rented cottage in the town about a mile and half away from the house and now war was openly declared between them. Solicitors were engaged and the battle over the house became as vicious as the battle over the pregnancy.

Emma was glad now that she had always insisted they keep separate bank accounts, sharing one only for household expenses. She had more than enough to buy Matt out of the house and maintain a mortgage on her own. She was good at what she did and highly successful and sought after. In the time they had lived in the house she had fulfilled another of her dreams and had been writing her first novel and to her delight, she had now secured a two book deal with a well-known publishing house. She was under pressure to meet the deadline which was at the end of September but since the divorce battle had begun, she'd found herself writing less and less, anxious about the future, knowing she needed to make a success of her novel in order to secure her and her baby's future and hold on to the house she loved so much. She was not afraid of being a single mother. She knew her own strengths and she knew she would always make good money in her first career but the money that would come from a successful writing career would enable her to comfortably buy Matt out of the house and live well for the foreseeable future.

Emma was nothing if not disciplined and well organised. She determined to pull herself together and finish her book in good time in order to secure the house once and for all. Pushing aside her concerns, each day thereafter she rose early, writing until lunchtime, then after a short break to eat, she would write again until early evening and so it was with a sense of relief and pride that the book was finished on time. She was thrilled when it was hailed an enormous success. Her agent assured her it was going to be a best seller and she found herself engaged in a whirlwind of meetings, public readings and book signings. Her future and that of her baby were secured and she couldn't have been happier. Matt on the other hand, was infuriated even further. He refused to congratulate her and grew ever more spiteful and vitriolic in his demands. Even his solicitor, well paid as he was and with every reason to want a protracted case, tried to talk some sense into him, failing miserably. He was determined that Emma would not hold on to the house.

As the year wore on and autumn turned into winter, Emma began to relax a little. Her own solicitor had assured her that as she was pregnant a judge was likely to look favourably on her wish to remain in the house, especially as she now had more than enough money to buy Matt out twice over and he was clearly just being very unreasonable. Emma had nodded in agreement, *Spiteful, is what I'd call it,* she thought to herself, *spiteful and nasty. I can't believe I ever loved him. I positively hate him right now. How could a man change so much in such a short space of time*? Had she ever known the real Matt? Back at the end of September she'd had to change all the locks, following a particularly frightening spat with Matt, who'd let himself in late one night, scaring her out of her wits when she found him standing over her bed, fists clenched and a look of pure hatred contorting his face.

"Give me the keys!" she'd yelled at him as he stood laughing at her impotency as she tried and failed to grab the keys from his outstretched hands.

"If you can take them from me, they're yours," he'd said as he roughly pushed her to the floor, callously disregarding both her and the baby.

Thoroughly afraid after this latest encounter, she'd also installed cameras and an alarm system but all this offered her little comfort and her nights were now routinely disturbed by a recurring nightmare. She would be standing out on the balcony, watching a storm tossed sea hurl angry waves at the shore. The wind would be howling like a banshee and the rain would lash her face but still she stood, rooted to the spot, looking out into the inky blackness until it appeared on the crest of a particularly large wave. She would watch, as the angry sea hurled a large suitcase onto the shore. Her dream self would then suddenly be on the beach, looking down at the battered case, broken open by the force of the landing on the sodden sand and it was with absolute horror that she would see a female corpse, curled like a foetus, crammed into the case. It was always at this point that she would awaken, screaming in terror and drenched in sweat, in a tangle of bedclothes.

She would spend the rest of the night roaming the house, checking doors and windows and trying to calm herself, sleep now a forgotten luxury. She tried to reason that the nightmares were simply a result of her anxiety over Matt and the vendetta he was now so obviously waging against her. Once the divorce was finalised she reflected now, he would disappear from her life for ever and the dreams would stop. Wistfully, she would wonder if they'd ever really loved each other. How could they have and now be such bitter enemies? How could the man she'd loved enough to marry have turned into such a callous monster simply because she'd changed her mind about wanting a baby? She understood that he hadn't wanted to change his mind and she respected that but surely she had the right to change hers without his becoming so hateful? Not for the first time she asked herself if she'd ever really known him. She was beginning to think not but she did now feel a twinge of guilt and shame at her own behaviour over the pregnancy. 'Still,' she told herself yet again, 'he thought it was an accident so he's being completely unreasonable. I'm not begging him to stay or to pay for a baby he doesn't want.'

By the second week of December, the weather had turned for the worse and there had been several blizzards. The view from her windows had taken on the look of a Christmas card and the snow was several inches deep. She was exhausted, not just from her pregnancy which was now in its eighth month but also from lack of sleep. Night after night, she would wake shaking with horror as she looked down on that poor body, long dead and cast aside like rubbish. She could make no sense of it no matter how long she dwelt on it. It was surely just a manifestation of her anxieties over Matt and the divorce. The happiness she had felt had long since evaporated and she felt she was living in a constant state of anxiety.

Mercifully, she hadn't seen Matt for months, not since he'd been warned by both the police and his solicitor to leave her alone or face arrest. Instead, he'd taken to phoning her and either breathing heavily down the phone or screaming at her that he'd never give her the house, that she was a selfish bitch and he had as much right to as she did. If he couldn't have it neither would she. He was still determined it would have to be sold and he would get his share. She would calmly reply that'd he would take it over her dead body.

Just before Christmas, the weather had settled and although it was still bitterly cold, it had stopped snowing and a calm peace had descended. Earlier that day she'd received the good news that the house was hers. The money to buy Matt out had been transferred and the divorce would be finalised, uncontested later in the new year. She had no idea why Matt had suddenly capitulated and she didn't care enough to dwell on it for long. Perhaps he had simply tired of the constant arguments or maybe the large sum of money recently deposited in his account was enough to assuage him. He could take time out, go travelling, buy a new car, do anything he liked with that amount of money.

Now, for the first time in days, the winds no longer howled around the house, whistling eerily in the eaves, making her shiver despite the warmth of the central heating and she was glad of the peace and quiet that ensued. After a long, soothing bath one evening, she took a cup of hot chocolate to bed, hopeful that now things were settled, she would get a full night's sleep and that the nightmare would not reoccur. She had not long switched off the lamp before she thought she heard the sound of breaking glass. Clumsily, she heaved her cumbersome body out of bed and as she reached the top of the stairs, she was shocked to see Matt already half way up.

Emma turned and ran back to her room but Matt had already made up the space between them and grabbing her by the throat, he squeezed hard and as she struggled to breathe she watched in terror as his face contorted with hate as he snarled at her.

"Did you really think you'd get away with your little plan to trap me? Do you really think I'm so stupid I didn't work out what you'd done, you, lying, treacherous, bitch! You said you'd only leave this house over your dead body. Well, I'm happy to oblige."

It was several days before Emma was missed and several months more before her body was found, the wind howling as if Tisiphone, Alecto and Megaera had all unleashed their fury at once. She was curled up like the foetus she had been carrying, in a large battered suitcase, abandoned on the shore by an angry, storm tossed sea.

The Rocking Chair

The Gables, when first I saw it, took my breath away. If a house can be described as magical, then this one, was indeed magical. I'd go further and call it enchanting. Comprising of three floors, the three large rooms to the front of the building on the ground floor, had huge, mullioned bow windows. The windows to the other floors, while also mullioned, were sash but large nevertheless. I recall thinking I was glad I didn't have to clean them. The grounds were well maintained, neat lawns and pretty borders and the drive leading up to the front door was just as neat, swept clean of any debris. This was a well-loved house, from the outside at least.

The interior, to my delight, proved to be no less beautiful. The inner porch opened into a magnificent hallway with a large, spiral staircase which swept up to the first floor. The three rooms with the lovely bows were tastefully furnished, in keeping with the age of the house itself, built I later learned, in the early eighteen hundred. The last of these, was a wonderful library, two walls of which were ground to ceiling book cases and there was a large, dark wood desk and green leather chair suggesting work as well as pleasure in this room. The old fireplace was stunning, but then they all were and I imagined the roaring fires burning at night, keeping out the worst of the chills large rooms like these must endure.

Eighteen months later, engaged to be married now and well familiar with the house and its inhabitants, my future in-laws and the youngest of their four children, Charlotte, I had agreed to stay over to take care of the teenager while her parents were away on business. My fiancé was unable to be there due to commitments of his own but I was sure Charlotte and I would rub along nicely; we'd always got on whenever we'd been together before and besides, she'd be at school for the first week of my stay, not breaking up for the Christmas holiday until the nineteenth of the month and her parents would be returning on the twenty-first, so as a trainee teacher, well used to classes of noisy teens, I was confident I would cope. I would fill my days reading, studying and simply enjoying this wonderful house. The decorations were already up and I was definitely in the Christmas spirit with college having closed for the holidays a full week earlier.

It had been snowing steadily for days so I was relieved when I finally pulled into the driveway and parked up. I had no intention of driving anywhere for the next few days. I knew the large, walk in larder and the fridge freezer would be well stocked and it was a fairly short walk to the local shop if I desperately needed anything not already thought of. Despite the central heating, I planned to light the fire in the large, airy sitting room and stay cosy indoors.

I would be using one of the two large rooms on the very top floor. Apparently, these had once upon a time been used by servants (I'd laughed when Adam had told me that but he'd assured me it was true). Charlotte's room was one of five on the first floor and was tucked out of the way, along a corridor and at the back of the house. At least, I had an ensuite so I wouldn't have to descend to the large family bathroom on this floor. At the time, the isolation of the attic room didn't bother me and I rather liked it. It had two of the lovely sash windows and a double, wrought iron bedstead was positioned between them. There was an exquisite patchwork quilt and I imagined it would offer perfect warmth on these chilly, winter nights. The furniture was, like the rest of the house, very old, solid, dark wood. The requisite fireplace was smaller than those of the large reception rooms but it was still rather lovely and it was a working one! To the right hand side, facing the windows, was an old fashioned rocking chair. I fell in love with the room instantly and felt I'd be quite comfortable and at home in it. I was actually looking forward to climbing between the sheets and snuggling down beneath that beautiful quilt.

Leaving my bags to be unpacked later, I returned to the ground floor and went into the kitchen. When the family were all at home, this was the hub of the house. Spacious and delightfully old fashioned (no modern cabinets here), the focus of the room was the huge, black Aga which heated this lovely old room and produced hearty meals. In the centre of the room stood a solid oak, farmhouse style table and chairs. The butcher's sink looked out over the rear gardens and at the back of the room was the door, leading to the walk-in larder and also to the cellar.

After perusing the freezer, packed with neatly labelled tubs and bags, I fetched a cottage pie and returned to the kitchen to make a cup of coffee. Biscuits and drink in hand, I made my way, to the sitting room and settled down to enjoy a magazine in front of the fire I'd lit a little earlier, savouring the aroma of the burning wood. Charlie, as she was affectionately known by the family, wouldn't be home for several more hours and I was looking forward to some quiet 'me' time. Engrossed as I was in the magazine, the dull thump I heard hardly registered at first but the second, louder one made me jump and I sat up, startled and listened intently for a few seconds before I decided to go and see if I could discover what had made the noise.

Everything in the hallway seemed normal and I was sure it hadn't come from the kitchen which was too far away. I peeked into the second room, which served as the dining room and here too all seemed as it should be. I expected to find nothing unusual in the library either, so when I opened the door and found several books lying on the wood floor, I hardly knew what to make of it. I peered behind the door but found nothing there and it was all quiet now. I moved into the room and walked to the window; it was closed and locked and although it was a cold day, with frequent flurries of snow, I could detect no discernible draft. How had the books fallen off the shelves on to the floor? Puzzled, but definitely not concerned, I picked them up and replaced them where I could see spaces from which I assumed they'd fallen. Returning to the sitting room, I put more wood on the fire, switched on the tree lights and returned to my magazine. Charlie came home a little while later and I began preparing our meal. Pouring myself a glass of the fine Chablis I had been told to help myself to, I listened quietly while Charlie moaned about the homework assignment she'd been given that day.

"Seriously," she groaned.

"It's less than a week until we break up so why can't he just cut us some slack? This is going to take me all night!"

I smiled and said that it was a teacher's job to make their students' lives miserable.

"Only kidding," I added.

"I'll help if I can and I'm sure together we'll get through it without having to stay up all night!"

Charlie grinned, thanked me and disappeared to change out of her uniform before dinner. The delicious aroma filling the kitchen was making me hungry and I was looking forward to the hearty meal that was soon to be on the table. I congratulated myself that I had landed such a fantastic task; a beautiful house, great wine and delicious meals I had not had to slave over a hot stove to prepare. Christmas carols played quietly in the background as I laid the table and dished up just as Charlie reappeared.

"I'm starving," she informed me as she flopped down onto a chair, scraping it towards the table, making me wince, reminding me as it did, of chalk on a blackboard.

"Just as well there's plenty here then. Tuck in," I said.

Our meal was a relaxed affair as we exchanged small talk; the pie was delicious, we agreed, the weather was suitably seasonal, Charlie couldn't wait for her holidays to begin, we both still had Christmas shopping to do. The kind of genial small talk enjoyed around dinner tables everywhere.

"Something really odd happened to me today," I finally said, "I heard strange noises and when I looked, some books had fallen off the shelves onto the floor in the library."

Charlie laughed.

"Ah," she said, "that's Mabel, our resident, friendly ghost. She's harmless."

A ghost? Was this Charlie's idea of a joke? Adam had never said his family home was haunted.

"A ghost," I said aloud, "are you having me on? I don't believe in ghosts."

"You will after a few nights here," she said, nonchalantly, "Mabel usually introduces herself in her own way and in her own time but there's really nothing to be scared about. Like I said, she's harmless. She just makes her presence felt by moving stuff around. Dad often finds his books in piles on the library floor and Mum never knows when her pantry's going to be reorganised! She likes to play tricks on us all."

She seemed to be serious and I took a large gulp of wine before asking who Mabel was. Apparently, she had been a servant in days gone by and according to Charlie was buried in the local churchyard. I was sceptical of the whole story, convinced Charlie was having me on and that there must be a logical explanation for the event earlier that afternoon. After all, no one else in the family had ever mentioned Mabel and I'd certainly never experienced anything out of the ordinary during previous visits. True, I'd never stayed overnight before but still, I was not convinced by Charlie's ghost, friendly or not.

"I'll look forward to meeting her."

I joked and began clearing our dishes.

"We never see her," Charlie said, "we only hear and see what she's done. I'm going to start my homework unless you want me to load the dishwasher?"

I told her I'd manage, adding that she'd only to ask if she wanted help with her homework and she disappeared upstairs, leaving me to clear up which took little enough time. I was going to head back into the sitting room to enjoy the fire and some TV before bedtime so I turned to fill up my wine glass, only to find it was full to the brim. *Strange,* I thought, *I don't remember doing that.*

That night I slept like a baby. Just as I'd thought it would be, the bed was comfortable and the quilt snug and warm and I woke refreshed and ready for breakfast, a simple affair of poached eggs on toast, juice and piping hot coffee, after which Charlie headed off to school. Once I'd cleared the breakfast dishes away I decided to head out for a walk. I'd made my mind up to visit the churchyard and see if I could find Mabel. As it happened, it wasn't difficult as it was rather small. The church was small too, typical of churches up and down the country. There was a lychgate and a few trees and my immediate impression was that there hadn't been any recent burials here; the grave stones all looked old and weathered. My guess was that most burials now took place in the larger cemetery at the other end of the village and many of these tombs had the sad air of neglect.

The air smelled crisp and fresh and despite my first impressions, it all looked rather pretty, covered as it was in a fresh layer of newly fallen snow and to my delight, there were snowdrops everywhere I looked, peeping up above the snow, under the trees and in clusters on the lawns. I remember thinking how odd it was that there should be so many of them at that particular time. Didn't they usually blossom in spring? I'd seen them as early as January before but in December? Still, they were an unexpected pleasure and it was incredibly peaceful; I was rather moved by the beauty of it, neglected or not. I spent some time reading the inscriptions on the headstones, wondering about the lives of those buried beneath. Some inscriptions told of lives long lived, other sadder stories told of those cut short or not begun at all and I felt tears prick at my eyes.

I found Mabel near the church itself, in the shadow of one of the trees, bare of leaves of course but clothed instead by snow covering its branches. Her gravestone revealed she had died in eighteen ninety-two at the age of fifty-nine. Mabel Barton had been a loving wife and mother and now slept 'peacefully in the arms of the Lord'. I stood quietly for a few moments before plucking a few snowdrops from the grass and placing them on the bare grave. It was clear that no one had visited Mabel in many years. The thought saddened me a little but the story was clearly repeated many times over; this little churchyard was the last resting place of people long dead and forgotten.

"Merry Christmas, Mabel," I said and left them all to their eternal rest.

I was glad to get back as it was freezing out and I felt chilled to the bone by now. A cup of coffee and a chocolate biscuit in hand, I retreated to the sitting room. The heating was on but I decided to light the fire anyway. I switched on the Christmas tree lights and settled down to watch a Christmas film. The day passed uneventfully and I was glad when Charlie came home and we sat down to our evening meal together, chatting easily about this and that.

Several hours later I was ready for bed, tired and looking forward to the warmth of the quilt and a good night's sleep. I drank the cup of hot chocolate I'd taken with me as I read a few pages of my book but when I realised I'd read the same line several times over, I switched off the lamp and snuggled down beneath the covers. I remember thinking I could smell something sweet, struggling to identify it but I had no time to dwell on it as I was asleep almost instantly.

I woke with a start, aware that it was still dark and the room had turned cold, the heating turned off some hours earlier. I lay still in the dark, listening and heard the strange, rhythmic sound that I knew without doubt was the chair, moving gently back and forth on its rockers. I reached out and switched on the bedside lamp and sure enough, there it was, the chair by the fireplace, gently rocking to and fro. I watched it for several moments, unafraid, curious even, wondering if I was dreaming. I have no idea how long I lay still, watching and listening, before drifting back off to sleep. I knew no more until the alarm clock's shrill call announced it was time to get up. I recall now the moment of surprise when I realised the bedside lamp was still on. I sat up and stared at it for a second or two before remembering the events of last night. I leapt out of bed and walked to the fireplace. The chair was quite still but there, on the cushioned seat, was a single snowdrop. I picked it up, lifted it to my nose and enjoyed the fresh, cool, familiar scent of the night before.

"Thank you, Mabel," I said smiling, as I turned to make my way downstairs to make breakfast and tell Charlie that I'd changed my mind about ghosts.

Good News

I very much doubt that, throughout the ages, there has ever been a funeral which can be described as anything other than difficult for those gathered to say goodbye to a loved one, a friend or a colleague. This one was no different, the icy November weather only adding to our misery. My poor mum had been inconsolable for days and it was awful to watch her now, struggling with her grief. Auntie Maggie was her eldest sibling and had essentially replaced the mother who had died whilst Mum was still quite young. She had been an enormous part of my life too as I'd never known my maternal grandmother and Aunt Maggie was indeed the matriarch of our family and although I was grieving also, I was more concerned with Mum. Dad was being stoic but he really didn't know how to cope with this and I could see how uncomfortable and helpless he felt. We watched sadly as the coffin, topped with wreaths from the family was lowered into the ground and the priest intoned the ancient words of burial and then the final goodbye before we all trudged back to the carpark and the waiting cars.

I had stayed on for a couple of days afterwards but then had made the two-hour drive back from my parents' home in Newcastle to our house in the Lake District, a little village further along the coast from Whitehaven, our toddler daughter Laura safely harnessed in her seat in the rear of the car. The journey across country via the A69 had given me lots of time to think about recent events. We had known it was coming but that hadn't made those last few days with Aunt Maggie any easier. I was glad I'd been able to be there and I know Mum was grateful for Laura's presence, her innocent babbling and enthusiasm for just about everything she saw and touched, a welcome distraction while we adults waited for the inevitable.

Laura was sleeping peacefully now and I replayed it all over and over, especially the last few minutes when mercifully my beloved aunt had slipped away and was free of her pain. Startled, I realised I wasn't really concentrating on the road and forced myself to do just that, my sleeping daughter the only incentive I needed to put my thoughts to rest and concentrate on the twisting, winding roads of rural Cumbria. By the time, I pulled up onto our driveway I was exhausted and Laura, now wide awake was grizzly and probably hungry.

Stu came out to carry her inside while I carried our bags and I recall feeling so fatigued all I wanted to do was fall into bed and sleep. Stu clearly saw how tired I was and said that I should go and lie down and he would take care of Laura. Not for the first time I was thankful for such a thoughtful, loving husband. He'd spent days on his own, put in a full day's work, cooked us a warming meal and now he was taking charge our very fretful toddler. Gratefully I crawled under the duvet, taking time only to kick off my shoes and letting the tears fall, I curled into a ball and waited for the blessed relief of sleep.

It was late when I woke up, the night sky dark and foreboding and I realised I'd been asleep for hours. I could hear the TV from the living room directly below our bedroom and hungry I decided to get up and join Stu downstairs. He smiled as I entered the living room, the only light coming from the TV screen and one, small lamp, sitting on a table in the corner of the room.

"Hungry?" he asked, getting up and folding me in his arms while I nodded against his chest.

"Sit down. I'll heat your dinner up. Won't be long," he said, disappearing into the kitchen, returning a short while later with a hot meal and a glass of my favourite Pinot.

We sat in companionable silence while I ate my Spag Bol, his signature dish and despite myself I couldn't help teasing him.

"How many times did you have this while we were gone?" I asked, putting my empty dish on the coffee table and picking up my wine glass.

He shrugged and smiled at me.

"Not sure, maybe five or six," he estimated.

"But in my defence, I did make sure I put a different veg in each time."

"We were only gone ten days!"

I slapped him playfully on his arm.

"You really need to expand your repertoire, my love, but thanks, it was delicious and honestly I could have eaten a horse."

Despite my earlier nap, I was tired and after a few small sips of wine, the last I would enjoy for quite some time to come, I placed the half full glass on the table and we headed upstairs to bed. I slept fitfully, visions of Aunt Maggie and conversations we'd had over the years replaying in my dreams. Her voice, so clear, so real replaying one of our last conversations before she'd slipped into merciful unconsciousness, 'Look after each other,' she'd urged me, her voice frail and weakening, her poor, skeletal hand gently lying in mine. 'Your mum will need you to be strong but she'll be fine in time. All she'll need is her family and something to look forward to and she'll get past this.'

I had promised her we'd look after each other, not really paying much attention to the rest of it but I woke with a start and recalled the conversation word for word. I lay in the early morning light thinking about it. Christmas was only five weeks away and Mum had always loved the festive season so hopefully her mind would be occupied with that. It had already been agreed that we would go to stay with my parents so having Laura about, especially at such a magical time would be just the pick me up she needed.

Later that morning, with Stu gone to work and Laura playing quietly with her toys, I dialled my parents' number, Dad picking up almost immediately, as if he'd been waiting by the phone for it to ring.

"Hi, Dad, how's Mum? Did she get much sleep?" I asked, knowing the answer before I'd even asked the question.

"Not well, pet," he replied, "she tossed and turned and I could hear her crying at times. She's napping now and I'm going to try and get her to eat something when she wakes up."

"I wish I could be there, Dad," I told him, "but it won't be long until we come home for Christmas. I'm sure she'll be alright soon. It's still early days and she and Aunt Maggie were so close, it's bound to be hard for her."

I promised to ring again the next day unless Mum wanted to talk me, in which case Dad promised he'd get her to ring later.

Scooping up Laura, I popped her into her snowsuit (no snow yet but the sky was dark and threatening) and strapped her into her car seat. Fifteen minutes later, we were sitting in the doctor's surgery, a nurse helpfully keeping Laura occupied while the doctor examined me.

"Congratulations."

Dr Sydney beamed at me.

"You are indeed pregnant, about eight or nine weeks but a scan will give us a more accurate timescale."

I was thrilled to have the confirmation – I had done a home test before I'd left for the funeral – and this visit to the doctor was just to have it made official. I drove home on cloud nine. We'd been trying for a second baby for a while and had suffered the agonising disappointment of a miscarriage early in the summer so although I was excited and I knew Stu would be too, this would be our secret until we arrived safely beyond the twelfth week. I decided Christmas Day would be the perfect time to reveal our news and this would be the perfect present for Mum and Dad, better than anything I would wrap up in jolly Christmas paper.

The following days dampened my joy somewhat, not because of the morning sickness that was now making its presence firmly felt, but because I was becoming increasingly concerned about Mum. She sounded so down and Dad couldn't hide his own concern from me, reporting that she had no appetite, that she wasn't sleeping and still cried too much for his comfort. I suggested he make an appointment for her to see her own doctor, telling him she may need anti-depressants and sleeping pills just for a time. He'd agreed he would discuss it with her and let me know what she said.

That night I had a really vivid dream. Aunt Maggie and I were sitting in a garden, the scent of roses, her favourites, filling the air, the shade of a tree sheltering us from the hot summer sun. She was holding my hand and smiling at me.

"Such good news," she said, "just what your mum needs. This will perk her up, you'll see."

I woke to find it was still dark outside and played the dream over in my head. How I wished Aunt Maggie could have been here to meet our new baby. *How strange to dream of her telling me she knew about our good news,* I thought and drifted back off into a dreamless sleep.

I was in the kitchen making Laura her breakfast when the phone rang. Dad didn't give me a chance to say anything other than 'Hello' before he began to speak. He sounded so much more upbeat than last time we spoke and I could only listen in silence as he explained the inexplicable.

"Well, you'll never believe this."

He began.

"I woke up in the middle of the night and your mum was sitting bolt upright talking to the bottom of the bed. Jessie, what are you doing? I asked her but she shushed me and said she'd tell me in a minute so I lay there listening to her one sided conversation. It didn't last long but when she lay down again she told me that your Aunt Maggie had come and given her a good talking to. She'd told her it was time to stop grieving because she was happy where she was and that at the end they'd all come for her, your grandparents and your Uncle Jim and that when it was her time, they'd be there for her too. Then she sat up again, turned to look at me and said but the best bit was that we have a lot to look forward to because Lucy has some good news."

There was the briefest of pauses before Dad said, "Lucy, are you pregnant?"

I almost dropped the phone and then I began to laugh, only now recalling that dream of us in the summer garden.

"Bloody hell, Dad," I said, "I only had it confirmed yesterday and I was going to tell you on Christmas Day but Aunt Maggie has beaten me to it!"

Dad, my strong, no nonsense dad, began to cry and finally said, "Well I never. I didn't believe in ghosts but I think I've just changed my mind."

"Me too, Dad," I told him, "me too."

Premonition

The nightmare was always the same. She was running uphill, along a path bordered on either side by dense woodland. She was running as hard and as fast as she could but getting nowhere and he was there, behind her in the darkness, a faceless creature, chasing her and she could feel the terror as he closed in on her and her efforts to outrun him were in vain. Should she get off the path, veer into the woodland, hide in the dark depths of the trees and hope he wouldn't find her? Her dream self never got the chance to do that because just as the faceless being reached for her, the knife raised to strike, she would wake, shaking and breathless, her heart pounding in her chest and the sound of her terror drumming in her ears. Each time she would have to crawl out of the warmth of her bed and grope her way to the bathroom. Each time she would have to sponge herself down, the sweat born of terror, trickling down her face, her neck, her back. She would peel off her nightgown or pyjamas and after the cool water soothed her overheated body, she would dress in fresh nightclothes and crawl back into bed, finally falling into a deep, dreamless sleep.

Each morning, she would wake and recall the night terror and ask herself the same question. What did it all mean? Why was her dream self being terrorised by an unseen man who wished her harm? Her life was pretty damn good, thank you very much. She had a good job as a paralegal in a well-respected law firm. She had a great flat in a good area. She had a close knit group of friends and a loving, supportive family. What on earth did it all mean? She had read somewhere in the distant past that dreams usually had meaning; the usual ones about teeth falling out, or running about naked in public but this was very different. It was terrifying and always left her drained and confused.

After yet another disturbed night, Molly lay curled up in the warmth of her duvet and allowed herself the luxury of time. She had the day off and was meeting friends later for lunch and some Christmas shopping. There were still five weeks until the big day but she had no more holiday time and she hadn't bought anything as yet. This would be a good time to start, the rest she would have to do on Saturdays and they were always busy so she fully intended to make the most of today.

She loved Newcastle city for shopping, the hustle and bustle of Northumberland Street and the yearly Christmas display in Fenwick's windows. People came from miles around to see it, queuing patiently with their children to walk past the animated display. Then there was Eldon Square Shopping Centre where you could find just about everything and anything you needed.

The drive along the coast road was busy but she didn't mind. She would still be in good time to meet Helen and Freya. She parked in the multi-story in Eldon Square and walked into the indoor centre to the arranged meeting place, a coffee shop in the central mall. Helen was already there and had managed to bag a table, no mean feat at this time of year. She waved and joined the queue for coffee, Freya arriving just as she reached the front, the delicious aroma of coffee beans and chocolate assailing her nostrils. She ordered the usual for them both – Helen already had her drink and was enjoying a slice of what looked like chocolate cake and then joined her friends at the table near the rear of the cafe. They chatted happily over their drinks and planned out the rest of their day. Shopping, lunch, Fenwick's window and more shopping!

They were on their way out of the cafe when Molly caught sight of him. He took her breath away. He was sitting at a table by the window, nearest the door and he was heavenly! She thought she recognised him from somewhere but couldn't put her finger on it and as it was just a fleeting glance as she followed her friends out into the mall, she didn't have time to dwell on it.

They made their way into the busy shopping centre and joined the Christmas crowds. The lights, the decorations, the shop window displays were admired and commented on. Freya liked the tree in the central square best. Helen adored the nativity scene while Molly loved it all.

"They always make a great job of it, don't they?" she said as they entered the little Christmas shop called The Christmas Box.

It was open all year round and Molly often wondered how much business they did at other times of the year. It was busy today though and they had to squeeze past excited children and stressed mothers to browse the displays. Molly picked up an angel clearly designed for a tree top.

"Look at this, girls."

She held the angel up for her friends to admire. It had a white dress with tiny silver stars on the bodice. Her wings were outspread and edged with silver too. Her halo sat atop her golden hair, which tumbled in curls about her neck. Her arms were held low, her palms facing outwards, her head slightly bent, as if she were perhaps looking at the baby in the manger.

"She's angelic."

Helen smiled as she reached out to touch the gossamer dress.

"Very astute!"

Molly laughed at her friend.

"She is an angel after all."

"It's gorgeous," Freya said, "do you need a new one?"

"It reminds me of the one we had for our tree at home," Molly said. "Mum always said it represented the Angel Gabriel and that he was the Virgin Mary's guardian angel. She told us we all had one too and that they watch over us wherever we go. She used to say that we'd know if our angel had come because we'd find a white feather. She taught us a prayer to our guardian angel and we used to say it every night at bedtime. I can still remember it, even now."

She mused as she held the glittering angel, admiring the way the little stars flashed as they caught the light. She decided she had to have it. It would make a lovely change to the star that had graced the top of her tree for the last few years. As she made her way to the till, she caught sight of him again near the door and he seemed to be looking directly at her, a smile on his handsome face and then he was gone. She craned her neck, trying to catch sight of him, see which way he had gone but he had disappeared into the crowds outside.

She realised with a little start, that she was disappointed. She would really like to speak to him, find out where she knew him from because she was now convinced she had seen him before. *Oh well*, she thought, *hopefully we'll bump into each other sooner or later.*

By four o'clock, they were all tired but happy with their purchases and having said their goodbyes and arranged their next meeting, they went their separate ways. It was growing dark and the drive home was no less busy than the drive in. Molly found herself thinking about the handsome stranger. She couldn't get his face out of her mind. She struggled to think where she had first seen him but try as she might, it was no clearer by the time she parked at home.

She unpacked her shopping and put everything away except the angel. She wouldn't be putting up her decorations for several weeks yet but she decided to keep it out and placed it on her bedside table. She stood quietly, admiring it again and feeling strangely light-hearted and went to shower before making herself a meal.

Several glasses of wine, a chicken tikka masala and a rom com later she was tired and ready for bed. She glanced again at the angel and climbing underneath her duvet, she switched off her lamp and lay quietly in the darkness. She expected to have the nightmare now, it was an almost nightly occurrence but that didn't stop her praying every night that her dreams would be pleasant ones. She thought again about what she'd told her friends in the shop.

"Can't hurt, can it?" she whispered.

> *Angel sent by God to guide me,*
> *be my light and walk beside me;*
> *be my guardian and protect me;*
> *on the paths of life direct me.*
> *Amen.*

Unfortunately, her prayer went unanswered, as she was once more chased by an unknown assailant but this time, as he was about to strike, a second stranger appeared from nowhere and stepped between them and her attacker fled. Just as her saviour turned to face her she woke, an overwhelming sense of disappointment washing over her. This was a new development but what did it mean and who was her hero? Only as she drifted back off to sleep did she remember saying the prayer and wonder what if?

The following few nights developed a pattern. She would touch the little angel on her head, crawl into bed and whisper the prayer. Each night, the chase began and just as she was about to look into the face of her saviour, she woke up. He remained tantalisingly out of reach.

The following Saturday she'd arranged to meet Helen and Freya in their favourite gastro pub but first she decided to clean the flat and put up her decorations. She retrieved the angel from her bedside and putting her into place on the top of her tree, she switched on the lights and stood back to admire the fruits of her labour.

"Not bad," she said aloud, looking at the angel, "you're definitely an improvement on the star."

She set off for her girls' night in a buoyant mood; she loved Christmas and it was her birthday the next day, hence the celebration meal. Her taxi arrived promptly and twenty minutes later they pulled into the car park of The Old Mill. She asked the driver if he could pick her up again at 11 p.m. and after paying him, she walked into the festively decorated pub. Helen and Freya were already there waiting for her. They'd ordered a bottle of Prosecco and as she sat down Helen poured her a glass.

"You look nice," she said, passing the glass, "is that top new?"

"Thanks, glad you like it. I've had it a while but it's the first time I've worn it. You both look good too but then we always do, don't we?"

She smiled at her friends and they all raised their glasses in a toast.

"To always looking good," Molly said.

"And a happy birthday for tomorrow!" Helen said.

"And a merry Christmas to us all," Freya added.

They ordered their meals, chatting happily about plans for the holidays, work and boyfriends.

"Maybe Santa will bring me a nice Prince Charming for Christmas."

Molly joked.

"I've been a good girl after all and after the last cheating, lying rat, I think I deserve one."

"Definitely," Freya said and Helen nodded her agreement. "Are you sure you don't want me to ask Paul if he has any nice friends?"

"I can vouch for dating apps."

Helen added, "I haven't looked back since I met Jake."

Molly sipped her Prosecco and smiled at her friends.

"Thanks, guys but honestly, I'm a great believer in 'if it's meant to happen it will', so I think I'll leave it to fate." She took another sip from her glass and then said, "I'm having the strangest dreams, well nightmares actually, I suppose. It's odd because I'm running away from a man, not trying to hook one!"

She told them about her nightly disturbances and how it had changed once she began saying the prayer.

"Wow, what do think brought them on?" Freya asked.

"I have no idea," Molly replied, "don't dreams mean your subconscious is trying to tell you something?"

"I think so," Helen said, "but I don't think they're meant to be taken literally. I'm sure this one is maybe a sign you're stressed, worried about something."

"I can't think of anything that's stressing me, except maybe being single."

She sighed.

"It could be a premonition," Freya said, "I don't mean you're literally going to be attacked."

She added this hurriedly, when Molly looked shocked.

"But, maybe it's a warning to be careful, to be alert, on your guard."

"Now I am spooked," Molly said, taking a large gulp of wine and replenishing her glass.

"I'm sure it's nothing to worry about," Helen said, "but if they carry on much longer, maybe you should see someone."

Their meals arrived and the subject was dropped as they ate and chatted about their works' Christmas parties, plans for Christmas Day and New Year's Eve. By the end of the evening, they were all in good spirits and more than a little tipsy. Their bill paid, they left the pub together and went out into the icy December air. Helen and Freya were sharing a taxi back into the Newcastle suburbs but Molly's taxi hadn't arrived yet.

"You two get off."

She urged them.

"I'm sure it will be here in a minute."

They hugged and she waved them off and watched as their taxi's lights disappeared around a bend in the road. She stood hugging her arms about her and stamping her feet against the cold. It was freezing and she hoped her taxi would be arriving soon. She turned towards the carpark to check again and decided to walk across and wait there as she'd arranged, having briefly considered going back into the pub to wait in the warmth but then deciding against it as she didn't want to miss its arrival, which should be imminent. It was quiet and despite the lighting from the pub, it was quite dark and gloomy. The taxi definitely wasn't there yet and she turned to walk back towards the light of the entrance to keep moving in a vain effort to warm up. She didn't hear him approach, and it was only as he pushed her to the ground, grabbing her bag that she realised she'd been followed across the dark carpark. He must have been lurking in the inky shadows at the edge of the carpark, waiting and biding his time for someone alone, just like her. She screamed and tried desperately to hang onto her bag, refusing to let go and then he was there, pulling her assailant off her and helping her to her feet. The mugger ran off into the night and she gasped out her thanks just as her taxi finally arrived.

"Thank you so much," she said, "I was really in trouble there for a minute."

"Will you be OK now?" he asked. "Do you want to call the police?"

"I don't think there's much point," she replied, "I didn't see his face and he's well out of the way by now."

"If you're sure," he said, opening the taxi door for her, "goodnight, stay safe."

She thought she heard him whisper, 'God bless,' as he closed the door and she looked up at him through the window. It was him, the guy from the shopping mall and then he was gone. She looked about her, twisting in her seat to see where he had gone but there was no sign of him. He had vanished into the darkness as quickly as he had come.

Shaken but otherwise unharmed, she locked the door behind her and got ready for bed. She was exhausted and still the worse for too much wine but she didn't want to go to bed just yet. She dreaded being alone in the darkness and the thought of the nightly terror after her near escape earlier, chilled her to the bone. She switched on her tree lights and the TV, hoping to distract herself but try as she might she couldn't get the thought of what had happened out of her head. She'd had a lucky escape thanks to her unknown but timely hero. Where had he disappeared to? One minute he was there, the next he was gone. She closed her eyes and pictured his face as she'd looked at him through the taxi window. It was definitely the same guy she'd seen in the mall. She knew she had seen him before and as her eyes rested on the angel she suddenly knew. She had seen him at her First Holy Communion, she had seen him at her confirmation and he had been there when she'd been rushed to hospital as a teenager when her appendix ruptured. An overwhelming sense of peace descended over her; she felt safe and finally able to go to bed. She switched off the TV and as she stood up after switching off the tree lights, something brushed her cheek.

She reached up and caught it and was completely unsurprised to see the purest white feather in the palm of her hand.

"Thank you," she whispered and switching off the lights went to bed, confident that her dreams would be pleasant ones from now on.

Red Ribbons

Pulling her scarf up to protect her nose from the icy wind, Callie stood at the little wooden gate and stared at the cottage beyond. Not exactly chocolate box pretty but nevertheless better than she had anticipated. A decent sized garden, mainly comprising two overgrown lawns, led up to a double fronted, two story building which now belonged solely to her.

The news that she was now the owner of a cottage had come out of the blue and was an unexpected but pleasant surprise. She'd heard of her great uncle William but had never met him and her knowledge of him was sketchy at best. She knew he was from her father's side of the family and that he had never married and had no siblings. Her father had once told her he was the black sheep of the family but had not expanded and she hadn't pressed him further, not much interested in a distant relative she'd never met.

The solicitor had simply told her she was the only named heir, the cottage was mortgage free, insured for the next year and that all that was needed was to sign the papers in front of her and the cottage would be officially hers. She had no intention of living in it; it was too far from her job and besides she was a city girl, used to the bright lights, restaurants and shops of London where she was a junior architect in a large firm. She had weighed up the options open to her. She could rent it out and have a steady extra income or sell it and enjoy the lump sum. As she stood now, looking at it through her architect's critical eyes, she was still undecided.

"Not bad, not bad at all," she said aloud, "especially as I didn't pay a penny for you."

She had taken a week's holiday and travelled to the village in Hampshire where the cottage was located. She'd been surprised to find it so isolated; she'd had to drive right out of the village and was glad of her car because the nearest shop was in the heart of the village itself and at least a mile and a half away. Surrounded by countryside, there wasn't another building in sight and she shivered, acknowledging it wasn't only the biting wind chilling her bones. The isolation was somewhat unnerving.

The front door opened onto a small central hallway, the staircase to the left. There was a door leading to a reasonable sized sitting room which looked out onto the front garden. It was fully furnished but old fashioned and definitely not to her taste. The hallway led to a kitchen at the rear and to the left, under the stairwell, another door opened onto a dining room, again fully furnished with a solid dark wood table and six chairs. Upstairs were two double bedrooms and a bathroom which while usable, could do with being updated. Still, it was hers and she couldn't help feeling excited. This cottage would bring in a little windfall either through rent or selling and that was welcome news. The beds were fully made up but she was glad she'd decided to bring her own pillows and bedding. There was dust on every surface and she shuddered at the thought of climbing between the fusty bedding. Her own would smell fresh and clean.

There was no gas, being so far out of town but the electricity was working and the oil fired central heating soon began to warm the icy rooms. She'd need to check on how much oil there was. She hoped it would be enough to get her through her short stay because it was December and the weather was typically cold and wet; she couldn't afford to be without heating.

Once the car was unpacked she set about remaking the bed in the bigger of the two rooms. She liked the dual aspect and the view from the rear window was particularly pleasing to the eye. In the distance, she could see hills with trees below and fields stretching for miles. She stood for a while, enjoying the view and then opened the window. The rooms smelt musty, not surprising really as the cottage had stood empty for several months. It seemed counterproductive to have put the heating on but she welcomed the blast of cold air and the rooms desperately needed to be aired.

Returning to the kitchen, she unloaded the groceries she'd wisely brought along and then dampening a cloth she set about wiping down the counter tops and the small table and chairs. The kitchen, like the rest of the house was old fashioned. It would need updating by whoever bought it, if and when she decided to sell. If she decided to rent as a holiday let, it would just about do with a lick of fresh paint. After several hours of cleaning, she was tired and hungry so she heated up a microwave ready meal and taking a glass of chilled Sauvignon into the living room, she decided to watch some TV before bed and to ring her boyfriend, Luke as promised.

"Hi," she said as soon as he answered, "I got here safely and it's not too bad, a bit old fashioned but in good condition.

It's a bit isolated though so I can't wait for you to get here. It's a bit spooky to be honest."

"I'll leave as early as I can on Friday. I've taken the afternoon off so I should be there early evening. Will you be OK until then?"

"I'll have to be, won't I?"

She sighed.

"It's only a couple of days. I'm sure I'll survive 'til then."

They chatted a while longer and when they'd hung up she flicked through the channels, finally settling on an old Miss Marple mystery. She was dozing, hard work and several glasses of wine ensuring she was unable to keep her eyes open, when a loud noise brought her instantly back to her senses. She sat for several seconds, startled and still fuzzy from sleep. Everything in the room appeared normal, the TV playing quietly in the corner so she got up and went out into the hallway. She switched the light on and stood listening for any stranger sounds. Nothing. The kitchen too was as it should be but when she went into the dining room she was surprised to see one of the doors on the sideboard was wide open. Could that explain such a loud noise? How did it open by itself? She shivered despite the heat from the nearby radiator and looked around the room for any other signs of disturbance. She walked to the window and looked out but it was pitch black outside, no moonlight able to pierce the dark clouds threatening rain. She pulled the curtains, shivering again and went over to the sideboard. Kneeling, she peeked into the little cupboard and pulled out an old photograph album. The only other stuff in there was a pile of papers, envelopes and newspaper cuttings so she closed the door firmly, pondering again how it could have opened and made enough noise to disturb her from a different room and took the album back into the living room.

Pouring herself another glass of wine, she began flicking through the photos. Most were shots of the countryside, hills, fields, a river and she wondered if they were of nearby scenes. A few showed a dark haired man sporting a beard and she stared at the handsome face thinking this must be her uncle as a young man. There were several more in which he had aged, his hair and beard white now and the handsome face looked less friendly and she struggled to put a word on the look on his face in several of the later shots. Angry? No, she decided, it was worse than that. Shuddering, she slammed the book shut. Malevolent, evil. He looked evil. Chilled to her bones, she threw aside the album and several loose photos fell out. She picked them up and stared at two pretty little girls. Both blonde, they looked to be about six or seven years old and both were clutching a doll. Each doll had a red ribbon in its hair, mirroring the ribbons in the girls' blonde locks. Who were they? They were standing in front of the cottage, holding hands. The only information about them was written in black ink on the reverse, their names presumably, Alice and Ava. Callie stared at the little faces from a time clearly in the distant past. Their clothes, hair and shoes all suggested the sixties but it was their faces which stood out as Callie stared at the old, creased photos. They both looked terrified. Who could these little girls be and why did they look so afraid? She was still considering the possibilities as she climbed the stairs to bed.

She snuggled beneath the duvet and exhausted from the day's activities she was soon asleep, her rest troubled by strange dreams of little girls with red ribbons in their hair. They appeared to be in a large, gloomy room, sparsely furnished and with only a skylight through which a pale moon offered the only light. They were crying and pleading with a tall, dark haired man whose face couldn't be seen.

"Please give us back our dolls," they wailed, "we'll be good, we promise."

The room disappeared and in her dream she woke with a start to find two, glassy eyed dolls staring at her from the foot of her bed. Callie gasped, a strangled cry in her throat and opened her eyes, not daring to look at the foot of her bed. She lay, staring up into the darkness. It was pitch black. No moonlight shone through the open curtains and there were no street lamps to lend their comforting glow. She lay rigid, listening to the silence. She couldn't move, fear and confusion robbing her of her senses for what seemed an unbearable eternity.

"It was just a bad dream," she said aloud, needing to hear the reassuring words, even if the voice was her own.

Tentatively, she reached out and groped for the light switch. The lamp on the bedside table flooded the room with its welcome glow and she scolded herself for being so foolish. There were no dolls, no sobbing girls, just the bedroom exactly as it was when she'd fallen asleep.

When she woke the next morning, the bedside lamp was still on and groggily she reached out to switch it off. She'd managed to fall asleep again but she hadn't been brave enough to plunge herself back into the dark. There'd been no more dreams and she lay now, still tired from her broken sleep. She shrugged into her dressing gown and hurried downstairs to switch the heating on. Maybe Luke would be able to work out the timer when he got here. It had defeated her yesterday and she'd finally given up, wishing she'd opted to leave it on overnight. One of her jobs today would be to determine how much oil there was in the tank. She switched the kettle on and put some bread in the toaster. She tuned into some festive Christmas carols and planned out her day while she ate her breakfast. First was the oil check, then she was going to start clearing out cupboards before venturing into the village to replenish groceries.

She was relieved to see the gauge on the oil tank read three quarters full, more than enough for the time she'd be here and she decided she could afford to leave the heating on tonight. She ventured into the kitchen and began sorting through the cupboards and drawers. Most stuff was serviceable and she decided on the dining room next. She was relieved to see the sideboard doors all firmly closed and laughed at herself. 'What did you expect?' she asked herself. Still, she wasn't sure she liked this room and quickly closed the door. 'I'll do this room when Luke gets here.'

The living room was just as she'd left it last night. Her wine glass was still on the small dark wood coffee table and the discarded photo album lay on the sofa where she hastily abandoned it. She picked it up, shuddering despite the warmth of the heating. She looked about her and realised there was little she could do in this room. There were no cupboards to sort through in here and as she'd cleaned yesterday she decided she'd postpone going through those upstairs and head out the village instead.

The weather was foul; it was raining heavily and to make matters worse there was an icy wind and she was grateful when she reached her car, parked outside the gate, there being no driveway. She was about to drive off when she thought she saw a figure in one of the bedroom windows but when she looked again there was nothing there. She pulled away looking back at the cottage through the rear view mirror but there was nothing to alarm her and she shrugged it off as her imagination, probably because she was tired and shaken from her nightmare.

She found a small carpark behind a row of shops on the unoriginally named Main Street and walked backed around to the shops, holding onto her hood as the wind tugged at it. She made her way quickly into the little general store and picking up a basket made her way around the aisles. Satisfied she had everything she needed for the next few days, she took her basket to the checkout, thanking the assistant who didn't even bother to look at her. Wandering back out into the rain, she had little desire to browse the shops but her attention was caught by the festive display of the little flower shop on the other side of the road. She crossed over and admired the creativity of the arrangement and the cheerful Christmas blooms. Impulsively, she decided what the gloomy cottage needed was some festive colour. She could take them back to London with her so they wouldn't be wasted. Christmas was still three weeks away but some poinsettia and sprigs of holly and mistletoe would bring some much needed cheer to her current surroundings.

Happy with her purchases she drove back to the cottage, hoping the rain would ease up. It was doing little to improve her mood and the skies remained ominously dark and brooding. She found herself praying for snow and then laughed at the absurdity. Snow was definitely not coming any time soon. She parked up, cursing that she'd need to make several trips to and from the car to unload everything she'd bought. By the time, she'd unloaded everything she was soaked to the skin. She hung her dripping coat on the stand behind the front door and headed upstairs to change. She hadn't unpacked her case the night before but once she was in dry clothes she decided she may as well hang up what few bits and pieces she'd brought with her. The old fashioned wardrobe was empty but there were a few hangers, sufficient for her trousers and blouses. She'd only brought three jumpers and these, along with her underwear she would put in the chest standing on the wall opposite the window. She opened the top drawer which was empty and placed her underwear inside. She fully expected the second drawer to be empty too but when she opened it, she found several rolls of red ribbon. She stared at them before picking one up, running her fingers along the silky strip. It was really beautiful and good quality but what on earth would an old bachelor want with such a lot of red ribbon? She shuddered, recalling the photo and her dream. She turned around, a sudden feeling of being watched and was relieved to find herself alone. She shoved the reel of ribbon back into the drawer and checked the one below; empty. Hurriedly, she put her folded jumpers in here and scurried back downstairs.

Unnerved by her discovery, she switched the radio on welcoming the cheery voice of the radio presenter announcing the next Christmas Carol. She unpacked her shopping, placing a couple of red poinsettias at either end of the window sill. She put the rest in the living room but what she needed right now was a cup of coffee and a sandwich. The holly sprigs would look great on the mantle above the fireplace and she'd hang some mistletoe just inside the front and back doors. Feeling more settled and slightly ridiculous, she decided she could even make use of the red ribbon. It would look fantastic wound around the banister.

After her lunch she took the remaining three poinsettia tubs, the holly and the mistletoe into the living room. She'd discovered a log pile in a small shed out the back garden and she thought it would be cosy to light a fire after she'd finished her decorating. She placed one plant of the little occasional table by the sofa, another on the window sill and the last on the coffee table situated between the sofa and the hearth. She carefully lay the holly along the mantle and stood back to admire the effect. She wished there was a tree and some lights but the short stay didn't warrant going to too much trouble and at least it was a little cheerier and festive now. She hung the mistletoe above the doors and then went upstairs to retrieve some ribbon. After a little effort, the banister was adorned with the deep red satin and she managed to affect a bow at the bottom by using another strand. She was rather pleased with herself and decided a little reward was in order.

She poured herself a large glass of wine and returned to the living room. It was dark outside, the afternoon drawing on and not helped by the black rain clouds still unleashing their venom on the world below. She switched on the little table lamp and pulled the curtains shut before picking up the stack of papers she'd brought in earlier from the dining room. There was nothing of much interest. Old bills, a few bank statements and appointment cards. She was about to put them to one side when an old, yellow newspaper cutting caught her eye. She read it with growing horror and then frantically searched the album for the photo of the two girls. She looked from one to the other, checking the description in the paper against the image in the photo. There was no mistake. The little girls in the photo matched the description of the abducted girls in the article and there was no mistake about their names. Alice and Ava, two friends had disappeared from a playground. Despite a frantic search, there had been no trace of them. The article was dated 20 August 1967 and stated that the search would continue, although after several days, hope was fading.

Callie sat, unable to move, her mind whirring. The girls in the photo were the missing girls and putting two and two together she concluded that her great uncle William had been the one who had abducted them. What other explanation could there be? They had clearly been here; the photo was taken at the front of the cottage but what had he done with them? Where were they? The only other newspaper cutting was from several months later and this stated that the search had been called off. The girls were still missing. Shaking, she picked up her phone and called Luke, begging him to come as soon as he could. After she explained what she'd found and her strange dream the night before, he promised he'd set out immediately and call work to explain he needed the extra time off. It was only a morning he'd miss; he was sure they would understand.

Relieved that Luke would be with her sooner than expected, Callie felt a little calmer. She gathered up the papers and photo and putting them and the album aside, she took a large gulp of wine and picking up her glass, she went back to the kitchen. She would make a meal for Luke, assuming he might be hungry when he arrived. She occupied herself making a lasagne, the delicious aroma filling the air and making her feel hungry too but she decided to wait and eat with Luke. Several glasses of wine later she felt more relaxed, chiding herself that she was letting her imagination run away with her. She didn't believe in ghosts and it was simply the realisation that her great uncle perhaps had a very dark history, that was leaving her so unsettled. Her father had called him the black sheep and she wished now she'd pressed him for more information but it was all moot because neither were still around to tell their respective stories. Once she'd taken the cooked dish out of the oven, she decided to take a bath. *She had time,* she told herself, *Luke wouldn't be here for another couple of hours.* He'd phoned several times to check on her and reassure her he was getting closer.

After a long, hot soak she put on some comfy pyjamas and her dressing gown and began to tidy her hastily discarded clothes, thrown carelessly onto the bed before her bath. Now she began folding them and was perplexed when she lifted the last of her clothes to find a spool of the red ribbon had been concealed underneath. *That's odd, I could swear I'd put that back in the drawer,* she thought as she lifted it off the bed and put it away. As she turned to leave the room she froze, the blood pounding in her ears, the hairs on the back of her neck standing on end. The door was closing of its own accord. She couldn't move. Terrified, she stood rooted to the spot and watched in horror as the door shut with a quiet click. Her need to escape overcoming her fear, she rushed to the door, pulling frantically in her desperation to get out of the room. For several long seconds, she pulled fruitlessly until she realised she needed to turn the knob instead. Flinging the door open, she sped downstairs, grabbing her car keys and coat and rushed outside to her car. Locking herself in, she gasped for air, taking long deep breaths until her pulse slowed and her heart beat returned to normal. She tried to rationalise what had just happened. The ribbon, the door. Surely there had to be a logical explanation. She was simply tired and unsettled by what she'd read. She had just forgotten to put the ribbon away. The door may have been caught by a draught. She was being ridiculous. Still, there was no way she was going back into that cottage by herself. She'd wait in the car until Luke arrived. Shivering as much from her recent experience as from the bitter cold, she switched on the engine and waited for the car to warm through. The radio was playing and the music helped calm her frayed nerves. Every now and then, she glanced at the cottage but all was still and despite herself, she struggled to keep her eyes open, dozing off to the soothing strains of Silent Night.

She was woken some time later, almost jumping out of her skin and could have cried with relief when she saw Luke's anxious face peering in at her.

"What the hell, Callie? Open the door. What are you doing out here?"

Callie all but leapt into his welcoming arms and allowed herself to be lifted and carried back into the cottage. Despite the events of earlier that evening, the warmth inside was a welcome relief and after Luke had made coffee and reheated the lasagne, Callie told him everything. He repeated what she had already told herself. It was simply what she had discovered about William and her mind playing tricks on her. They would do some research, get things in order and leave the place behind for good. God, this was just what she had needed. Calm, rational thinking. She laughed.

"You're right. I was becoming a bit hysterical there for a while. I mean, locking myself in the car. What an idiot."

Luke laughed too and kissing her lightly on the top of her head, said, "Come on, bedtime. You're exhausted and so I am. We can sort this all out tomorrow."

If she had hoped having Luke with her would ensure a sound night's sleep, she had hoped in vain. She was woken by a noise she struggled at first to identify but as she lay in the dark, Luke's quiet breathing beside her reassuring, she realised to her horror, that she was listening to the sound of footsteps running back and forth above her and that there were at least two pairs of feet making the noise.

"Luke, wake up," she whispered, shaking him, "there's someone in the attic!"

Groggily, Luke sat up, listening intently.

"I can't hear anything," he said, "you were probably just having another dream."

"It's stopped, but I wasn't imagining it," she told him, "the noise woke me up."

"Could just be mice," he said, pulling her into his arms, "they can be noisy little blighters. I'll go up and check tomorrow. Try and go back to sleep."

Luke woke her with a cup of coffee and poached eggs on toast.

"Come on, sleepy head, up and at 'em," he said, putting the tray into her hands.

"What time is it?" she asked, smiling at his thoughtfulness.

"Gone nine, but you were sleeping so soundly and you obviously needed it after last night."

He sat on the bed and looked at her.

"You, OK? You were pretty shaken last night. What do you want to do today? I can go up into the attic and check for mice. What else would you like to do?"

"I think I'll come up with you. I'd like to see for myself. I need to see evidence of mice with my own eyes."

After breakfast and several cups of coffee, she was ready to face whatever awaited in the attic. Luke pulled down the loft ladder and went ahead of her, helping her up through the hatch. They stood looking about them, coughing as they disturbed years of dust. The skylight above allowed very little daylight in, hardly surprising as the skies were yet again dark and foreboding. Luke found a light switch and fortunately the dust covered bulb still worked. He wiped the bulb clean and they began their search. Old bits of furniture and boxes were piled up around them. In the far corner, to the rear of the room, was a pile of what appeared to be heavy curtains. There was clearly something underneath and Luke pulled the weighty material aside, sending more dust motes into the air and causing them both to cough again, covering their mouths too late.

An old leather trunk, remarkably free of dirt and dust, had been hidden underneath. The straps were secured but not locked and Luke undid them, lifting the heavy lid up until it rested against the wall behind.

"Oh my God, Callie, don't look," he said, but it was too late.

Disbelief and terror coursing through her, she stared down into the trunk, her hands raised to her mouth as Luke put his arms around her. They stood, looking down at the horror before them. Two little skeletons, curled up like skinless foetuses, each with a doll in its skeletal arm and wearing red ribbons, not in their blonde hair, sad wisps still visible, but around their little necks.

Callie and Luke watched in silence as the police cars and pathologist left before they locked up the cottage and drove away. It was the second week of January before it was confirmed that the missing girls had indeed at last been found, the cause of death strangulation, confirmed by the autopsy, the culprit clearly one William Burnett, unfortunately deceased so unable to pay for his crimes.

Callie had decided never to return to the cottage, putting it into the hands of an estate agent who she had made promise would make any potential buyer aware of its history, although she truly believed there would be no stranger noises and disturbances. The girls had been found and they were no longer prisoners in that dusty attic room, in a cottage far from home, having endured unimaginable horrors.

The police had kept them informed of events and they were present when the little girls were finally laid to rest, family members thanking them for finding their long lost relatives, sadly their own parents all long gone, never knowing what had happened to their precious girls. Two families ripped apart by one evil man. Callie stood silently looking at the grave, the families deciding to keep the girls together and laid two bunches of pretty flowers, one for Alice and one for Ava.

"I hope you can sleep peacefully now," she whispered, "no need to cry and run about in that horrible attic."

Silently, she let the tears fall until she felt Luke take her hand and lead her away, leaving the girls to their eternal sleep, hoping and praying their sad little ghosts were haunt the cottage no more.

Lily

Lily stood, arms outstretched in a silent plea. Blood from the terrible gash on her brow, poured down her face, making her almost unrecognisable. She opened her mouth and screamed.

Ashley struggled towards consciousness, the scream her own and as she finally broke free of her drug induced sleep, the scream died on her lips and she began to sob, loud wails of despair and grief bringing the nurses running to her bedside. Calm hands and soothing voices, a sharp scratch as the needle pierced her skin and she sank back into the blessed relief of deep unconsciousness.

Ashley placed the bouquet gently on top of the grave. She'd chosen carefully; orange and white Calla Lilies. They'd always been her favourite, their mum's too and she had given her eldest child their name, Lily. Ashley had missed the funeral because by the time she'd left the hospital, her broken bones healed, if not her mind, her elder sister had been buried three months. She stood now, looking down at the freshly laid earth, tears falling unchecked down her frozen cheeks and wished yet again, that they hadn't got into the car on that fateful day.

It had actually been Lily's idea to drive the twenty or so miles into Leeds city centre to do some Christmas Shopping.

"Let's do it."

She'd cajoled.

"It'll be fun. We can have a nice lunch and the Christmas market is always great."

"OK, OK, I give in."

Ashley had laughed.

"But I'm driving. My nerves can't stand you at the wheel."

"Cheeky," Lily said, thumping her sister playfully on the arm, "I'm an expert driver!"

"You would give any racing driver a run for their money," Ashley had told her, "I'm driving or the deal's off!"

The weather was crisp and bright, there'd been an early frost but by the time they set off, it was clear and dry, though the temperature was a chilly six degrees. The roads had been gritted but Ashley kept her speed down and by the time they parked up in a multi-story in Leeds centre, they were in good spirits and ready to enjoy their shopping trip.

They made their way straight to the Christmas market. Lily was in her element. She loved all things Christmas and this was the perfect place to shop. The quirky stalls selling all things Christmassy as well as things like hand stitched gloves, pretty scarves and knitted hats. The lights, the noise, the enticing smells of cinnamon and nutmeg vying with frying onions from the hotdog stall; Lily loved it all. Ashley smiled at her sister's obvious delight. It wasn't that she didn't enjoy the season, she did but for Lily it was always just as magical as it had been when they were children. If she hadn't known better, Ashley would have sworn Lily still believed in the Tooth Fairy, the Easter Bunny and of course Santa Claus. She was like a little girl let loose in a sweet shop. Her excitement was infectious. Ashley caught her mood and they spent several happy hours browsing the stalls, each buying gifts for their mum and dad before deciding they were hungry and needed a break for lunch.

It was dark and the weather had changed for the worse by the time they set off home. Ominous clouds threatened an oncoming storm and Ashley decided to get off the main road and take a quieter, though slightly longer route home. Happy and relaxed, they were singing along to Christmas carols when rounding a bend, a car coming in the opposite direction, travelling far too fast and with full beams on, clipped their wing mirror. For a split second, Ashley was blinded and shocked by the contact, swerved wildly. She was conscious of Lily's panicked scream, the grating of metal scraping along tarmac, then nothing but blackness.

All during those long, agonising weeks in hospital Ashley was tortured by visions of Lily, her blood curdling scream and always the vision was the same. Her dreams were haunted by her sister, blood pouring down her face, arms outstretched pleading for help. The doctors, the family and the police all told her the same thing. It was an accident. It wasn't her fault. She was not to blame.

Once she was well enough to talk, the police had taken her statement and assured her and her parents that an investigation to find the other driver would leave no stone unturned. They would check for cars that needed new wing mirrors but they couldn't promise anything, they would keep them regularly updated. They never did find him and this only added to Ashley's anguish.

Ashley had returned to her parents' home, unable to face the flat she and Lily had shared. She didn't know if she would ever feel ready but it was too soon just now. It was her mother's comforting arms that held and rocked her each time the nightmare woke her, screaming along with Lily. It was some weeks later that Ashley remembered her parents too were grieving and her guilt multiplied and became unbearable.

By midsummer, after several months of intensive therapy, and with encouragement from her parents, she decided it was finally time to move back into the flat. Her mum helped her clean and freshen the rooms after more than six months of being left empty. She had offered to stay the first few nights but Ashley had assured her she needed to do it alone.

"I'll be fine, Mum, I promise. Everyone keeps telling me I need to get on with my life and you're right. Go home to Dad. I'll ring you this evening."

She kissed her mum on the cheek, hugging her and then closed the door quietly after watching her mum climb into her car. After her mum had left she wandered about the flat, reacquainting herself with the space she'd shared so happily with her beloved sister, going from living room to kitchen, to the bathroom, leaving Lily's bedroom until last. There was no trace of Lily left. Her parents, believing they were doing what was best for her, had cleared out Lily's belongings while Ashley had been staying with them. She understood their wish to protect her but she wished with all her heart they'd left Lily's things untouched. She stood in the doorway, desperately trying to feel some trace of Lily and trying her best not to cry but failing miserably, eventually giving in to the grief and curling up on the bed, she sobbed herself to sleep.

For the first time since the accident, her sleep was dreamless. When she woke, it was dark outside and she lay quietly for several seconds, until she realised where she was.

Lily, where are you? Where did you go?

She sat up, her head still groggy from sleep and waited another few seconds before she felt able to stand up. The flat was eerily silent and she walked to the window, peering out into the darkness. There was no moon, the sky dark and brooding. She realised she was hungry and wondered what the time was. She went through into the kitchen and fished out the quiche her mum had left in the fridge. Throwing together a salad to go with it and pouring herself a large glass of Shiraz, she went through into the little living room. Placing her meal and glass on the coffee table, she lit the lamps and gas fire, pulled the curtains and sat down wearily. Despite her hunger, she picked at her meal, struggling to finish it. The wine was a different matter and she went to the kitchen to replenish her glass, deciding to take the bottle back with her.

She sat in silence, drinking her wine until, the bottle almost finished, she fell asleep where she had curled up on the sofa. When she woke, the sky was growing light and she realised again that her sleep had been dreamless. No visions of Lily, no screaming and no feelings of hopelessness and guilt. The wine? She sat up, rubbing her stiff neck and moaned, her hangover already kicking in.

"Lily," she whispered to the quiet room, "I miss you."

She was thankful she was still on sick leave and padded through to take a shower, letting the hot spray ease her stiffness and soothe her aching head. The familiar scent of coconuts filled the air and Ashley closed her eyes, threw her head back and let the hot water cascade over her. Lily had always loved the smell of coconut scented toiletries and Ashley was glad that they had shared shampoos, conditioners and soaps because it meant that whatever else had been cleared out, this little bit of her remained.

"I'm so sorry, Lily," she said aloud for the zillionth time, "it should have been me."

Reluctantly, she got out of the shower, dried off and dressed.

She padded through into the kitchen. It was still only seven o'clock and the whole day stretched ahead of her. The thought filled her with dread. What on earth would she find to fill the lonely hours ahead? She needed company she decided and walked into the centre of the village to the Coffee Pot, the little cafe she and Lily had often frequented together. She knew the friendly staff well and some of the regulars too, although she enjoyed the fact that it attracted its fair share of visitors to the village. Dogs were welcome if kept on their leash and she liked the warm, welcome atmosphere. She found an empty table to the rear and took her latte and chocolate brownie, smiling at several people she recognised. One, an older man with a friendly smile always brought his cocker spaniel.

"Hello, girl."

She smiled and bent to stroke the silky fur. The dog wagged her tail happily and allowed herself to be petted.

"What's her name?" she asked, still stroking as the dog seemed to enjoy it.

"Pip."

The man smiled at her.

"She's a grand lass, great company. I don't know what I'd do without her."

Ashley relaxed a little and enjoyed her coffee and chat with Pip and her owner and went home with a new spring in step for the first time since the accident. I'm going to get a dog, she decided, I need company and something to focus on.

Three weeks later, she'd chosen a West Highland Terrier puppy who would be ready to leave its mother in another two weeks. Excitedly she started preparing for his arrival, buying a training crate, bowls, toys and food. She'd decided to call him Baxter and had a collar with her phone number on the tag, ready and waiting for his arrival. As she was putting his things into the kitchen unit especially allocated to him, she caught the faintest whiff of coconut. She stood up, spinning around.

"Lily? Is that you?" she said aloud, "You always wanted a dog. Do you approve?"

She waited silently, desperate for a sign of her sister's presence but the scent had disappeared as swiftly as it had come and there was nothing but the sound of her own heart drumming in her ears.

Baxter's training and care needs gave Ashley the much needed focus she craved. She walked him twice a day, rain, hail or shine. She brushed him, she talked to him, she cuddled him and loved him. He slept on her bed, despite her initial determination that he would have his own bed in the kitchen. She found it comforting to have his little body curled up next to her, to feel his warmth, to listen to the little noises he made and to have his unconditional loyalty and love. The terrible dreams of Lily had faded and eventually disappeared, though the grief and the guilt remained. Meanwhile, Baxter developed his own little character and Ashley enjoyed watching him play with his toys, scampering about in the park or simply sleeping, curled on her lap or next to her on the sofa.

It was several weeks after his arrival that she noticed he would suddenly sit still, alert, staring at nothing in particular, his little head cocked to one side and it was then she would catch the faintest whiff of coconut in the air.

Lily. She would whisper, 'You're here, aren't you?' She was comforted by it and wished she could see her and talk to her. She missed her still and as the year wore on the feelings of guilt and loss resurfaced and the nightmares began again.

She would wake, screaming in unison with Lily, Baxter licking her face anxiously. The scent of coconuts would be more noticeable than ever and as she hugged Baxter to her, she would beg Lily's forgiveness. She knew she was causing the little dog anxiety and this made her feel even worse.

"I'm so sorry boy."

She would hold him close, stroking his fur and burying her face in his little body.

"You don't know what's going on, do you?"

She tried to make up for the disturbed nights by giving him lots of attention and love during the day but the guilt and anxiety remained. Each time she hoped she was coming to terms with it all, each time she had a period of relative peace, it would all begin again.

She'd been back at work for a while now and Baxter enjoyed the doggy day care centre near her office. The staff assured her he was sociable and happy but still, she worried that her night terrors were adversely affecting him and this only added to her feelings of guilt. She found herself talking aloud to Lily more and more.

"Lily, I really am so sorry. I know they've all told me it was an accident, that it wasn't my fault but I wish you would give me a sign. Please, Lily, if you're here, please let me know it's OK."

She would wait, hoping for an answer but other than the occasional hint of coconut and Baxter staring at nothing in particular, there was nothing. She reasoned that as she still used the coconut scented toiletries, it was probably not unusual that she could smell them but she longed to believe it was Lily's presence and that Baxter could sense her too. After all, she told herself, dogs were supposed to be able to sense these kind of things, weren't they?

As the anniversary of the accident neared, Ashley's mood plummeted. She had no enthusiasm for Christmas preparations. She would be staying with her parents from Christmas Eve through to Boxing Day so she decided against putting up any decorations in the flat.

"Maybe next year, boy," she said to Baxter, "it seems disrespectful to Lily to celebrate too much this year."

The dreaded day finally dawned. Ashley got up early and then showered and dressed, she put Baxter's harness and lead on and picking up the bouquet of orange and white lilies she'd bought the day before, she set off to walk to the cemetery. She knew her parents would be going later in the day but she'd told them she would need to go earlier, making an excuse to go alone. She couldn't face their grief as well as her own. She gently placed her bouquet on the grave, looking sadly at the writing on the headstone. Such a promising life cut short. So young. Too young. Feelings of sadness and the ever present guilt overwhelmed her and she sank to her knees, sobbing as Baxter whined and anxiously licked her face.

"I'm sorry, boy, I'm sorry, Lily. I'm so useless. You both deserve better than me."

She picked Baxter up, snuggling into his fur and there it was, the familiar and comforting scent of coconuts.

"Lily, forgive me please."

She begged again and setting Baxter down, tears streaming unchecked down her face, they left the graveside and returned to the flat.

The day stretched ahead of her and she decided she would clean the flat and make herself a lasagne. She wasn't sure she'd have much of an appetite but it would kill some time. She switched the radio on, hoping the cheery carols would help lift her mood. She smiled as Baxter picked up one his soft toys and shook it from side to side. He at least seemed relaxed and she was glad that he was apparently unaffected by the day's melancholy.

She dusted the little sideboard, lifting the vase of lilies she'd bought along with the bouquet for her sister's grave. The strong scent they gave off overwhelmed her with nostalgia. Her mother always had a vase of lilies in the sitting room at home and she smiled sadly as she thought about her family, her childhood and now the first Christmas without Lily. She put the vase back down and went back into the kitchen to make the lasagne.

The day had seemed endless and at last she fell into bed, exhausted and thankful it was almost over. *Would it be easier next year,* she wondered, *or the year after that or the one after that?*

"I'll never, ever forget you Lily," she whispered into the darkness, "but please don't blame me for wishing it will get better. I'll always regret the decision to go shopping that day but I don't think I can live like this for much longer. Forgive me. I love you."

She pulled Baxter close, whispered goodnight to him and prayed for sleep.

As with every night for quite some weeks, she dreamed of Lily but this time, it wasn't the Lily immediately after the accident, screaming and bloodied. This time it was her laughing, bubbly sister, the sister who had always made her happy, feel loved and the sister she would miss until her dying day. Lily smiled at her.

"I love you, sis," she said and kissed Ashley's cheek and gave her a lily, a single white lily.

Ashley woke with a start, touching her cheek, brushing off an imaginary spider. She sat up, amazed that she had slept so soundly, the sky already lightening beyond the curtains. She swung her feet to the floor, sliding into her slippers and froze. On her pillow was a single white lily. She stared at it for several long seconds and then picked it up, the scent mingling with the strongest ever aroma of coconuts.

"Lily," she said aloud, smiling, "it's you. You're really here. I love you too. Baxter, come on, boy," she said, and went to the hall cupboard to pull out the Christmas decorations.

Ingram Content Group UK Ltd.
Milton Keynes UK
UKHW020626160323
418667UK00014B/1229